Perished by Pasta

A Simply Scrumptious Cozy Culinary Mystery Book

Tessa Aura

Copyright © 2024 by Tessa Aura

All rights reserved.

No portion of this book may be reproduced in any form without written permission from the publisher or author, except as permitted by U.S. copyright law.

Contents

The Murder	1
1. La Bella Tavola	2
2. Wines and Whispers	9
Connecting The Dots	18
3. Pepperoni's Lead	19
4. Marco's Involvement	25
5. The Bait	31
The Resolution	37
6. The Festival and the Trap	38
7. Aftermath and New Beginning	46
The Deep Dive	52
8. The Rival Chef	53
9. The Local Mafia	61
10. The Wealthy Tourist	69
Secrets and Connections	75
11. The Town's History	76
12. Marco's Past	81

13.	The Hidden Society	89
14.	Intensifying Doubts	99
15.	The Final Choice	102

The Murder

Chapter One

La Bella Tavola

"Pepperoni, hurry up. We must get back to La Nonna's Nonna." I pull his leash to stop him from sniffing around.

The sun begins to set over Cinque Terre, casting long shadows across the narrow cobblestone streets. The pastel-colored buildings that line the hillside glow warmly in the fading light, and the air is filled with the scent of the sea mixed with comforting aromas of fresh basil, garlic, and tomatoes simmering in kitchens all over town.

It's the kind of evening that usually makes me feel happy to be alive and grateful to live in such a beautiful place. But today, I can't seem to shake the restless energy buzzing under my skin.

Pepperoni, my mischievous beagle, trots beside me, his nose twitching as he sniffs out every possible scent on our evening walk. His floppy ears bounce with each step, and I smile despite myself. He's my little partner in crime—or, more accurately, a partner in solving crimes since trouble always seems to find me no matter how hard I try to avoid it.

"Come on, Pepperoni. It's been a long day, let's get home," I say tugging lightly on his leash. My trattoria, named in honor of my beloved grandmother, is just around the corner. After a long day of cooking, I'm more than ready to close shop, pour myself a glass of wine, and curl up with a good book.

But Pepperoni has other ideas. His nose suddenly catches a new scent, and he pulls me toward a nearby alley. I sigh but follow him, knowing better than to try and argue with a beagle on a mission.

The alley leads to the back entrance of La Bella Tavola, a sleek new restaurant that opened just months ago. The place has been trying to make a name for itself as the "next big thing" in Cinque Terre's culinary scene, but it feels out of place in our cozy, traditional town.

I've always thought the modern decor and fancy fusion dishes were too flashy for the local vibe. Plus, the owner, a haughty chef named Lorenzo, has a reputation for looking down on the rest of us "simple" chefs who still make food the old-fashioned way—with love and a lot of butter.

I'm about to pull Pepperoni away when I notice something strange. The door to the restaurant is slightly ajar, and there's a faint light coming from inside. My heart skips a beat. It's well past closing time for La Bella Tavola, and I know Lorenzo isn't one to leave things half-done. He's a perfectionist to a fault.

"Stay here, boy," I whisper to Pepperoni, though I know he won't listen. He follows me as I cautiously push the door open and step inside.

The dining area is empty, and the tables are neatly set with wine glasses and polished silverware reflecting the soft glow of the overhead lights. It's eerily quiet, save for the faint hum of the refrigerator in the back. Something doesn't feel right.

I take a couple steps into the room, my eyes scanning for any sign of life. That's when I see him. Sprawled out on the floor behind the bar, lying face down, is a man. I can tell immediately that something is very, very wrong.

"Oh, my...," I gasped, rushing over to him. My heart pounds in my chest as I kneel beside the body, my fingers trembling as I reach out to check for a pulse. But it's no use. He's cold. Lifeless.

And then it hits me. This isn't just any man lying dead on the floor. It's Alistair Fitzwilliam—the notoriously picky and snobby food critic who's been making the rounds in Cinque Terre for the past few months, terrorizing every restaurant he reviews—including mine—with his scathing commentary.

My breath catches in my throat as I stare at his lifeless form. Alistair was arrogant and unkind, but he didn't deserve this. No one does.

Pepperoni sniffs at the floor beside Alistair's head, his nose brushing against something small and round. A piece of penne, I realize, rolling my eyes at the absurdity of it all. Even in death, Alistair can't escape food.

"Pepperoni, no!" I scold, pulling him back just as he tries to nab the fallen penne. The last thing I need is for my dog to be munching on potential evidence.

I fumble for my phone, my hands shaking as I try to dial the local police. The phone slips from my fingers and I nearly drop it. "Get it together, Filomena," I mutter to myself. Finally, I manage to press the right buttons, and after what feels like an eternity, Constable Ricci answers.

"Filomena? What's going on?" His voice is calm but curious as if he's half-expecting me to call with a story about some minor disaster in the kitchen.

"Ricci, you need to get down here," I whisper, trying to keep my voice steady. "I'm at La Bella Tavola. It's Alistair Fitzwilliam... He's dead."

There's a pause at the other end, followed by the sound of rustling papers. "Stay where you are. I'll be there in five minutes," Ricci says, and then the line goes dead.

I let out a shaky breath and glance around the room, trying to make sense of what's happening. Alistair Fitzwilliam, dead in a restaurant? It's like something out of a bad mystery novel. And yet, here I am, right in the middle of it.

Pepperoni sits beside me, his big brown eyes wide and innocent, completely unaware of the gravity of the situation. I reach down and scratch behind his ears, more for my own comfort than his. "What do you think, boy? How does a food critic end up dead in the middle of a restaurant?"

Pepperoni doesn't answer, of course, but his nose twitches again, and he trots off toward the kitchen. I hesitate for a moment, then follow him. My instincts are telling me that something is off—something more than just a dead body in a restaurant.

The kitchen is spotless, which isn't surprising given Lorenzo's obsession with cleanliness. But as I step inside, I notice a small detail that sends a chill down my spine. One of the knives is missing from the magnetic strip on the wall. I know this kitchen layout well enough to recognize that every knife has its place, and the absence of one is obvious.

"Could this be the murder weapon?" I murmur to myself, eyeing the empty space where the knife should be.

***

Pepperoni, ever the curious beagle, noses around the base of the counter, his tail wagging as he sniffs out something interesting. I lean down to see what he's found—another clue, perhaps? But all I find is a crumpled napkin that smells faintly of olive oil.

Before I can investigate further, I hear footsteps approaching. Constable Ricci strides into the kitchen, his ever-present notebook in hand and a serious expression on his usually laid-back face.

"Filomena," he greets me with a nod, glancing around the room. "You seem to have a talent for finding yourself in the middle of things like this."

I give him a weak smile. "Believe me, it's not a talent I asked for."

He chuckles softly and then turns his attention to the body in the dining area. "Alistair Fitzwilliam," he mutters, shaking his head. "Can't say I'm surprised, given how many enemies that man's made in the last few weeks. But still... murder? In Cinque Terre? This is going to cause quite a stir."

I watch as Ricci kneels beside the body, examining the scene with a practiced eye. He's been the local constable here for years, and while he might seem easygoing on the surface, I know he takes his job seriously. He also has a knack for solving crimes, even if his methods are a bit unconventional at times.

"I found something," I say, pointing toward the kitchen. "There's a knife missing from the rack. Do you think it might be associated with the murder?"

Ricci raises an eyebrow and follows me into the kitchen, his eyes scanning the neat rows of knives until he spots the empty space. He lets out a low whistle. "Good eye, Filomena. We'll need to track that down."

He pulls out his notebook and starts jotting down notes, his brow furrowed in concentration. I can tell he's already piecing together the puzzle in his mind, trying to figure out who had the motive—and the opportunity—to kill Alistair Fitzwilliam.

I lean against the counter, watching him work. "Any ideas on who might have done this?"

Ricci shrugs without looking up. "Could be anyone, honestly. Alistair made many enemies in a short amount of time. It could be a disgruntled chef, a competitor, or even someone on his own staff. We'll have to dig into his background to see who had the most to gain from his death."

I nod, but my mind is already racing ahead, thinking of all the people who had a grudge against Alistair. There's Lorenzo, of course—he's fiercely protective of his reputation, and a bad review from Alistair could have been enough to push him over the edge. But then there's also Giovanna, a rival chef who's been trying to steal my customers for months. She's never liked me, and she had a run-in with Alistair just last week.

And what about Marco, the charming owner of the wine bar down the street? He's always seemed friendly enough, but I've heard rumors about his mysterious past. Could he have something to hide?

Pepperoni lets out a small whine, drawing my attention back to the present. I kneel beside him, rubbing his ears. "What do you think, boy? Who did it?"

Pepperoni, as usual, offers no answers. But I can't shake the feeling that this mystery is just beginning and that it's going to get a lot more complicated before we find the truth.

Ricci stands up, tucking his notebook into his pocket. "Alright, Filomena, I need you to head home for now. We'll be processing the scene, and I'll have more questions for you in the morning."

I hesitate, glancing down at Alistair's lifeless form one last time. "Do you really think you'll be able to solve this, Ricci? I mean, this isn't exactly a run-of-the-mill case."

Ricci gives me a reassuring smile, though there's a hint of seriousness in his eyes. "I've handled tougher cases than this, Filomena. Don't worry. We'll find out who did this."

I nod, trusting him even though I can't shake the feeling that there's more to this story than meets the eye. As I leave the restaurant with Pepperoni by my side, I can't help but think about all the people who might have had a motive to kill Alistair. Giovanna, Lorenzo, Marco... the list goes on. Alistair was hated by almost everyone in town. He never said anything good about the food, but murder seems a bit extreme.

Something else nags at the back of my mind. A detail I can't quite put my finger on. Something that doesn't add up.

As I make my way back to La Nonna's Nonna, the familiar scents of rosemary and garlic waft through the air, but tonight, they don't bring me the usual comfort. Instead, they remind me of the growing mystery surrounding Alistair's death.

I know I should leave the investigation to Ricci, but I also know that I won't be able to stay away. Not when there are so many unanswered questions. Not when someone in this town might be hiding a deadly secret.

And definitely not when there's a mystery just waiting to be solved.

As I close the door to my apartment above the trattoria, a mix of exhaustion and excitement settles over me. Tomorrow is a new day, and it's bound to bring more than fresh pasta and satisfied customers.

It's going to bring answers.

Or, at the very least, more questions.

And I'll be ready for them.

Chapter Two

Wines and Whispers

The morning sun filters through the windows of La Nonna's Nonna, casting golden rays onto the wooden tables and making the copper pots hanging in the kitchen glisten like they're brand new. Pepperoni is sleeping in his kennel, but my mind is racing with a thousand questions.

I've always loved this time of day—the quiet calm before the chaos of the lunch rush when I can prepare my ingredients, sip a cappuccino, and pretend for just a few minutes that the world outside these walls is peaceful.

But today, that peace feels far out of reach.

I'm distracted, my thoughts circling around the events of last night. The image of Alistair Fitzwilliam's lifeless body haunts me, and the more I think about it, the more I feel an overwhelming need to do something.

I can't just sit back and let Ricci handle the investigation—what if this murder casts a shadow over my trattoria? Everyone in town knows that I'm not a fan of him. In fact, I had gotten into an argument with him just last week. What if people start associating my beloved restaurant with death and scandal? I've worked too hard to let that happen.

With a sigh, I glance at the clock on the wall. It's early yet, but I know I won't be able to focus on prepping until I've at least tried to make sense of things. I'll head over to the market later and see if anyone's heard anything about the murder.

News travels fast in Cinque Terre, and someone is bound to have some gossip.

As I stir the simmering marinara sauce on the stove, the front door creaks open, and I hear the soft jingle of the bell above it. I look up, expecting to see Maria, my sous chef, arriving for her shift. But instead, standing in the doorway with a charming, easy smile and a bottle of wine in his hand, is Marco.

"Buongiorno, Filomena," he says in that smooth, velvety voice of his that never fails to send a little shiver down my spine. He steps inside, his dark eyes sweeping over the cozy dining room before landing on me. "I brought something for you."

Marco, the owner of the wine bar just down the street, is everything I'm not—calm, collected, and effortlessly sophisticated. He has this way of moving through the world that makes everything he does seem graceful, whether he's pouring a glass of wine or making small talk with customers.

Meanwhile, I'm constantly stumbling over my own feet, literally and figuratively.

I wipe my hands on my apron and smile at him. "Good morning, Marco. To what do I owe the pleasure?"

He crosses the room in a few smooth strides and places the bottle of wine on the counter with a flourish. "I thought you might appreciate a little something to help you through the day," he says with a wink. "It's a beautiful Barbera—full-bodied, with just the right balance of acidity and fruit. Perfect for pairing with your famous pasta dishes."

I raise an eyebrow, trying to ignore the flutter in my chest. "A bottle of wine this early in the day? Are you trying to get me tipsy before the lunch rush?"

Marco chuckles, leaning against the counter and folding his arms across his chest. "I wouldn't dream of it. But I thought you could use a little pick-me-up, considering the news that's been circulating around town."

I pause, my smile fading as I realize what he's referring to. "You heard about Alistair, then."

He nods, his expression growing more serious. "It's all anyone's talking about this morning. I heard from some of my regulars that he was found dead at La Bella Tavola last night. It's... unsettling, to say the least. I thought I'd come by and see how you're holding up."

There's genuine concern in his eyes, and for a moment, I forget about the mystery and the stress that's been gnawing at me. I forget everything except the way he's looking at me—like he actually cares about how I'm doing.

"I'm... okay," I say, though the words don't feel entirely true. I want to say more, to tell him how the whole thing has been weighing on me, but I hesitate. I've always prided myself on being independent. Admitting that I'm shaken feels like a weakness.

Marco doesn't press me, though. Instead, he reaches out and gently taps the bottle of wine with his finger. "Maybe you can save this for after the lunch rush then," he suggests with a small smile. "You can relax with a glass and try to forget about all the chaos for a little while."

I laugh softly, the tension in my shoulders easing just a bit. "Maybe I will. Thank you, Marco. You always know exactly what I need."

"It's a talent of mine," he says with a wink, though there's a sincerity in his voice that makes my heart skip a beat.

I glance down at the bottle, tracing the label with my finger. "It's strange, isn't it? Alistair being murdered like that. I mean, I know he wasn't the most popular person in town, but murder? It just doesn't seem real."

Marco nods, his expression thoughtful. "He had a way of rubbing people the wrong way, that's for sure. But murder... that's another level entirely. I can't help but wonder who could have hated him enough to do something like that."

"That's exactly what's been on my mind," I admit, turning back to the stove to stir the sauce again. "And I can't stop thinking about how this could affect my restaurant. What if people start associating La Nonna's Nonna with the murder? What if they think we're connected somehow?"

Marco steps closer, his presence warm and reassuring beside me. "Filomena, no one is going to think that. You have a reputation in this town—a good one. People know that you're one of the best chefs in Cinque Terre, and they love this place. One murder isn't going to change that."

I appreciate his words, but I can't shake the nagging worry in the back of my mind. "I hope you're right."

There's a brief silence between us, and I feel his gaze lingering on me. When I glance up, I find him watching me with a soft expression that sends a rush of warmth through my chest. It's not the first time I've caught him looking at me like that, but every time it happens, it catches me off guard.

Before I can say anything else, the front door jingles again, and Maria bustles in, her cheeks flushed from the morning air. "Buongiorno, Filomena! Marco! What are you doing here so early?" she asks, her eyes sparkling with curiosity as she glances between us.

Marco flashes her one of his signature smiles. "Just bringing Filomena a little gift," he says, tapping the bottle of wine. "I'll leave you to it, ladies. Don't let me keep you from your work."

I nod, giving him a grateful smile. "Thank you, Marco. I'll see you later?"

He holds my gaze for just a moment longer, then nods. "You will. And don't forget to enjoy that wine."

With that, he turns and heads for the door, leaving me standing there with a strange mix of emotions swirling in my chest. As much as I want to focus on the mystery of Alistair's death, I can't deny that there's something between Marco and me. And as much as I try to push it aside, I find myself thinking about him increasingly.

Maria watches him leave, then turns to me with a knowing grin. "You and Marco, huh? I've been saying for months that you two would make a cute couple."

I roll my eyes, trying to ignore the heat rising in my cheeks. "It's not like that, Maria. We're just friends."

"Friends with chemistry," she teases, waggling her eyebrows. "I see the way he looks at you. And the way you look at him, for that matter."

I open my mouth to protest, but the truth is, she's not entirely wrong. There is something between us—something unspoken but undeniably there. I just don't know what to do about it. My life is already complicated enough without throwing romance into the mix, especially when there's a murder to solve.

"Well, whether there's chemistry or not, we have work to do," I say, trying to change the subject. "Let's get the prep work done before the lunch crowd arrives."

Maria gives me one last knowing look but thankfully drops the subject. We dive into the familiar rhythm of chopping vegetables, kneading dough, and simmering sauces. For a little while, I manage to push thoughts of Marco—and Alistair's murder—out of my mind.

***

By the time the lunch rush hits, La Nonna's Nonna is bustling with the usual mix of locals and tourists. The air is filled with the comforting sounds of clinking silverware, sizzling pans, and the soft murmur of conversations. The smell of garlic and tomatoes wafts through the room, and I find myself falling into the familiar rhythm of running the kitchen.

But even as I move from station to station, checking on dishes and giving instructions to Maria and the rest of the staff, my mind keeps drifting back to the murder. Who could have done it? And why? Alistair had plenty of enemies, but murder... it seems so extreme.

Between plating pasta and tossing salads, I overhear snippets of conversation from the dining room. The murder is on everyone's lips. I catch fragments of gossip—speculations about who might have had the motive, whispered rumors about Alistair's past. It seems like everyone in town has an opinion, but no one has any real answers.

After the last lunch customer leaves, I finally take a moment to sit down and catch my breath. Maria is wiping down the tables, humming softly to herself. I pour myself a small glass of the Barbera that Marco brought earlier. The rich, deep red wine tastes like dark cherries and has a hint of spice. For a moment, I let myself savor the simple pleasure of it.

But the peace doesn't last long. My thoughts keep circling back to Alistair, to the murder, and to the feeling that there's something I'm missing. Something important.

I pull out my phone and start doing a bit of research, trying to find out more about Alistair's history. It doesn't take long to dig up some dirt. Alistair Fitzwilliam wasn't just a harsh critic—he had a reputation for destroying restaurants with a single review.

I read article after article about chefs whose careers were ruined after Alistair published his scathing critiques. Some never recovered.

One article mentions a French chef who had a breakdown after Alistair's review caused his Michelin-starred restaurant to close. Another tells the story of an up-and-coming chef in New York who left the industry entirely after Alistair's cruel words devastated her confidence. It's a pattern. Alistair didn't just critique food; he eviscerated people's dreams.

The more I read, the more I realize just how many people could have had a motive to kill him. Alistair wasn't just disliked—he was hated. There's a long list of chefs who might have wanted revenge. But who among them had the opportunity? And why here, in Cinque Terre, of all places?

I'm so absorbed in my research that I barely notice when Marco walks in. He's carrying a small box, which he sits down on the counter with a smile. "I thought you might like some fresh olives," he says, his voice pulling me out of my thoughts. "Picked them up from a friend of mine who has a grove just outside town."

I look up, startled, and then smile. "You always know how to spoil me, don't you?"

He grins, leaning against the counter. "It's not spoiling if it's just good hospitality. How's everything going? You look deep in thought."

I take a sip of my wine, hesitating for a moment before answering. "I've been doing some research on Alistair. Turns out he's left a trail of ruined restaurants behind him. There are dozens of chefs who have reasons to hate him."

Marco's expression darkens slightly, and he nods. "I've heard stories like that. He wasn't just a critic—he seemed to take pleasure in tearing people down. It's sad, really."

"Sad? I'd call it infuriating," I say, a bit more sharply than I intended. "He destroyed people's lives, and he didn't care. Maybe someone finally decided to give him what they thought he deserved."

There's a pause, and Marco studies me for a moment before speaking again. "You sound like you're getting involved in this, Filomena. Are you sure that's a good idea?"

I meet his gaze, feeling a mix of frustration and determination bubbling inside me. "I can't just sit back and do nothing, Marco. This is my town, my restaurant. If this murder casts a shadow over Cinque Terre, it's going to affect all of us. And I don't trust the police to figure it out on their own. Ricci is a good man, but he's not exactly Sherlock Holmes."

Marco's eyes soften. "I understand. Just..." he reaches out to gently touch my arm, "be careful, alright? I don't want to see you get hurt."

His touch sends a warmth through me, and for a moment, the world seems to narrow down to just the two of us. There's something in his eyes—something that makes my heart beat a little faster. But before I can say anything, Maria bursts into the kitchen, breaking the moment.

"Filomena, we've got a delivery at the back door," she says, oblivious to the tension in the room. "I need you to sign for it."

I nod, standing up and giving Marco a small smile. "Thanks again for the olives. I'll see you around, OK?"

He nods, his gaze lingering on me for just a moment longer before he turns to leave. As I watch him go, I can't help but wonder if there's more to Marco than meets the eye. He's charming, yes, but there's a part of him that he keeps hidden. A past he doesn't talk about.

And in a town like Cinque Terre, where secrets are as abundant as the olive trees, that makes me wonder what Marco might be hiding.

I shake my head, trying to push the thought away. I'm probably just overthinking things. But as I head to the back door to deal with the delivery, I can't shake the feeling that this mystery is only going to get more complicated—and that Marco is somehow going to be a part of it, whether I like it or not.

Connecting The Dots

Chapter Three

Pepperoni's Lead

As I walk back to the trattoria, I notice Pepperoni growling. I tug on his leash a bit, but his growling continues.

"Come on, Pepperoni," I say, tugging lightly on his leash. "We need to get back to sign for a delivery."

Pepperoni trots beside me, so curious, as he sniffs every surface. People don't understand how I can trust my dog so much, but ever since I got him, he has had a nose for clues. Not many people believe me, but I think he has a knack for solving mysteries, just like me.

We reach the trattoria's entrance, and I spot the delivery man emerging from the back alley. He's a wiry figure with a scruffy beard and a stained uniform that's seen better days. His eyes dart around nervously, and he clutches a brown, unmarked parcel close to his chest. The duffel bag slung over his shoulder seems out of place, too casual for a delivery uniform.

As I approach, Pepperoni's behavior changes abruptly. He stiffens, his ears perk, and he starts barking furiously at the delivery man.

"Woof! Woof!"

I am caught off guard by his sudden agitation. "Pepperoni, stop it!"

The delivery man glances down at Pepperoni, his face twitching with a mixture of annoyance and something else—a sense of unease. He seems reluctant to make eye contact, his gaze flickering from Pepperoni to me. There is something too calculated about his movements like he's trying to keep his distance.

"Sign here, please," I say, extending the receipt for him to sign.

He takes the receipt, his fingers brushing mine briefly. His touch sends an eerie shiver through me. He scribbles his name with practiced ease, then hands the parcel to me. The box is plain, nondescript—nothing that would hint at anything suspicious. I glance at the delivery man, who is making a concerted effort to avoid any further interaction.

"Thank you," I say, but he's already turning away, heading towards the alley from which he appeared.

Pepperoni's barking grows more insistent. I look down at him, puzzled by his extreme reaction. He's practically vibrating with excitement, his little body trembling as he watches the delivery man retreat.

"OK, OK, let's figure this out," I mutter, pulling out my phone to check the time. The delivery man has already disappeared into the maze of narrow streets, his figure swallowed up by the labyrinthine paths.

I decided to follow him. "Come on, Pepperoni."

We head out of the trattoria, and I can't help but notice how the delivery man's pace quickens as he navigates the winding streets. He glances back over his shoulder once, then picks up his pace even more. I push myself to follow, weaving through the twisting alleyways and trying to keep him in sight.

The narrow streets of Cinque Terre are both beautiful and treacherous, their cobblestones uneven and their turns sharp. I'm slightly out of breath, but the thought of losing the delivery man keeps me moving. Every time I think I'm gaining ground he takes a turn or slips into an alley that seems to appear out of nowhere.

I finally catch a glimpse of him ducking into a small, shadowed shop. The shop's sign is faded, and the windows are dusty, giving it an air of neglect. I slow to a stop, catching my breath as I peer through the shop's grimy window. The interior is cluttered, filled with old furniture and boxes stacked haphazardly.

I'm curious but hesitant. The shop doesn't seem like a usual stop for deliveries. I decided to investigate further. I push open the door and step inside. The air is thick with the smell of dust and age. The light filtering through the dirty windows casts a dim glow on the cluttered interior.

"Hello?" I call out, my voice echoing slightly.

No response. I make my way through the clutter, carefully navigating around piles of old newspapers and broken furniture. The shop feels oddly silent as though time has stood still within its walls. I spot a door at the back of the shop that's slightly ajar. I can hear faint murmurs coming from beyond.

I inch closer, my curiosity getting the better of me. I push the door open just enough to peek through. The delivery man is inside, talking to another man whose face is hidden in the shadows. Their conversation is too quiet for me to hear clearly, but the urgency in their voices is palpable.

Before I can fully comprehend what's happening, the delivery man looks up and catches sight of me through the gap in the door. His eyes widen, and he nudges the other man. The other man quickly heads towards a side exit, disappearing into the streets before I can react.

The delivery man, now seemingly trapped, looks at me with a mix of frustration and fear. He makes a half-hearted attempt to slip past me, but I block his path.

"Hey, what are you doing in here?" I yell, trying to sound composed despite the whirlwind of activity.

He shifts uncomfortably, his gaze darting around as though looking for an escape route. "I was just... taking care of some business."

I don't get a chance to probe further. He pushes past me and exits the shop with an urgency that leaves me standing there puzzled. I watch him disappear around the corner, my mind racing with questions.

Pepperoni trots over to me, looking up with his big, inquisitive eyes. I pat him on the head, trying to calm my own racing thoughts. "Well, Pepperoni, that was something. Let's get back to the trattoria and figure out what's going on."

As we head back, I can't shake the feeling that there's more to this delivery man than meets the eye. His behavior is far from ordinary, and the secretive conversation with the other man adds another layer to the mystery. Though I'm not yet sure how it all fits together, I know this encounter is a piece of a larger puzzle.

Back at La Nonna's Nonna, I take a moment to collect my thoughts. The package is now in my possession, but the delivery man's suspicious behavior has undoubtedly given me something to think about. I have to keep investigating, following every lead no matter how tangled they might be.

***

Hours later, I still can't get my mind off the delivery man and his strange behavior. No matter how much I try, I just can't brush it off. There was something suspicious about him.

His shady behavior makes alarm bells ring in my head. With all the people that Alistair had upset, I wouldn't be surprised if the delivery man, too, had some motive.

I am so lost in my thoughts as I try to figure out this mystery that I don't even hear the bell ring as someone enters my café. Pepperoni's bark pushes me out of my thoughts, and I look up, alarmed, before my eyes fall on Constable Ricci.

"Filomena! You seem lost," he says as he walks toward me, and I try to pull myself together.

"Yeah, I am sorry, but the whole thing with Alistair is haunting me. I can't stop thinking about what happened." I tell him, my mind still piecing together small clues to make sense of what had happened.

I guess that's the problem. The quote "curiosity killed the cat" applies to me in every way possible. Every time something like this happens, I get so involved in it just because I feel this incessant urge to solve whatever mystery there is.

"You seem to be more concerned about it than I am." Constable Ricci jokes, trying to lighten the mood. I try to smile at his attempt but fail, making him more serious, too.

"Is there anything new that you found, Filomena? What is bothering you?" he asks, his tone concerned.

I stayed silent for a moment, trying to figure out how to tell him what happened. Would he think I am being paranoid or reading too much into the situation? But then again, telling Ricci might help. He is a constable and might have more information than me.

"I followed this shady delivery man who was lurking around the alley for no reason. Pepperoni was going crazy over his presence, and when we caught up to the man, he looked scared of something." I tell him slowly, brushing a strand of my hair away from my face.

"A delivery man? Describe him to me." Constable Ricci's voice instantly becomes serious and alert.

"I am not sure, he kept his face down, but he had a scruffy beard and dirty clothes. He looked very suspicious." I tell him, trying to recollect more details about the man.

Ricci scratches his head. "That delivery guy? He has been around for years. A bit odd but harmless."

I wanted to feel better that he at least knew the man, but I still wasn't convinced. "Then why did he look so scared and nervous?"

Ricci sighs, rubbing the back of his neck. "Alright, I'll look into it. But we've got a long list of suspects already. Other people have more motive to kill the man than a delivery man."

I nod. He isn't wrong. With how many people Alistair had irritated, I wouldn't be surprised if someone more influential was responsible.

"I'm telling you, something's not right. I'll bet you ten servings of penne that this guy knows more than he's letting on." I insist, and Constable Ricci just nods understandingly.

"Thanks for telling me, Filomena. I will make sure I pay attention to this." He reassures me, and I smile at him gratefully.

We make small talk for the next few minutes before Constable Ricci takes his leave, but even after he is gone, I sit in my quiet café, feeling uneasy. But the case is far from solved, and I have no other option but to wait.

Chapter Four

Marco's Involvement

The next day is just as bad, if not worse. No matter how hard I try, I just can't get the murder out of my mind. It's like a curse that I am haunted with. All night, I stayed up trying to find a connection between the delivery man and the murder.

Constable Ricci is right; with all the people that Alistair had ruined, a delivery man does not seem like a big suspect. But despite what he thinks, this case affects me, so everyone is a suspect.

I want this case solved as quickly as possible. Not only is it a problem that Alistair and I got into an argument not long before his death, but the way people are avoiding eating out is seriously affecting my business, something I cannot afford.

I have worked too hard for my business to lose all its credibility and popularity because of someone else's crime.

My mind is still churning with all these thoughts as I pass through Marco's wine bar, only to find him casually leaning against the stone wall of the bar. Our eyes meet from the distance, and he straightens, flashing me his signature half-smile that makes all the local girls gush. I can't even act like I'm any different as it makes my own heart skip a beat. I wish I knew what it was between us, but for now, we haven't put a label on it.

And with everything going on, romance is the furthest thing from my mind.

I watch as he walks toward me and stops just in front of me.

"You look like you've seen better days, Filomena," Marco teases, his voice as smooth as the vintage Chianti he pours for tourists.

Something about the way he teases me makes me relax a little, the air around me lightening.

"That obvious, huh?" I sigh, impressed with his ability to read me.

"Considering you aren't as lively and talkative as you are normally when you leave your café, I would say so," he says as he takes a step closer. His eyes, which were glinting with mischief only seconds ago, are now softened by concern. "What's bothering you so much?" he asks softly.

I swallow a lump in my throat, feeling vulnerable as I look at him. "With the murder of Alistair, everything is becoming more complicated by the day. Because of my argument with him and my general involvement in the case, people are starting to avoid my café. I have worked so hard to make a name for myself. I have been tirelessly trying to find out the truth and clear my name. I spent yesterday chasing leads, but none of them seem to amount to anything. It's all very complicated, and I have no idea what to do anymore." I vent, unable to hold it in.

"Okay, that is a lot for someone to manage. How about we sit and talk?" Marco suggests, the concern evident in his voice as he leads me toward one of the benches nearby.

I go with him, sitting beside him as I try to pull myself together. I am not normally like this. I have always been fond of mysteries, and trying to find the answers has always been a calling. But this time around, I have so much at stake, and it is starting to take a toll on me.

"You are taking too much responsibility for solving this case, Filomena. I don't see how anyone here can suspect you, and even if they do, I am sure the authorities and Constable Ricci will eventually find the truth. Why are you putting so much pressure on yourself?" he asks, looking at me with a mix of concern and sympathy.

"I know, but I just can't sit around and wait for them to take their time. I already feel so helpless. It's my entire life's hard work at stake here, Marco. How can I just sit back and let it go to waste?"

I hate being vulnerable at this moment, but considering how messed up this entire case is, I have no idea how to react. I have come no closer to finding the truth, and with each passing day, the stakes become higher.

"Hey, hey." He murmurs, wrapping his arm around my shoulder. "It's going to be OK."

He watches me as I try to pull myself together, giving me the space to do so before he finally speaks again.

"It's obvious that you are not willing to let this smooth itself out. So, at least let me help you," he offers.

My eyes shoot to his; I'm shocked by his offer. Ever since Marco opened his wine bar here, he has been known for keeping to himself and strictly minding his own business. This is why most people consider him mysterious. The fact that very few people know anything about him makes everyone question his past.

Including me.

"You?" I ask, completely thrown aback by his offer to get involved in all this tricky business just for my sake.

He raises an eyebrow at my surprised tone before a small half-smile appears on his face again. "Aren't we friends? You have been going around investigating the case on your own for days now. The least I can do is help."

"But how can you even help?" My stomach flips at his words. It's not that he isn't a nice guy; it's just that I never got the impression that Marco cares about anything other than his own bar.

"Okay, now don't underestimate me so much," he says, his tone jokingly offended as he looks at me. "You'll be shocked by how much I know. Just because I don't actively involve myself in everyone's business, doesn't mean I don't hear what goes on."

The mood between us lightens as I shoot him a challenging look. "Oh, is that so? What is it that you know that I don't?" I have trouble believing that he knows more than me. I'm very social and always get the juicy gossip first.

"Well..." he starts before pausing to see if anyone is within earshot. Then he lowers his voice and tells me what he knows. "Did you know that Alistair died due to anaphylactic shock from consuming shrimp? Or that an extortion note was found in his pants pocket?"

"What?" I exclaim, completely taken aback. Nobody had told me anything about that.

He smirks at my reaction. "Still don't think I can be of any use?" he asks smugly, and I roll my eyes.

"Oh, come on, tell me how you know this?" I ask him, feeling rejuvenated by the latest information.

"I overheard Constable Ricci talking to one of his team members. They were discussing the evidence they had found. Apparently, somebody had been using subpar ingredients and Alistair found out. The note was a warning for him to keep his mouth shut."

With each new detail he shares, I become more intrigued. "Subpar ingredients?" I repeat, appalled. As a chef, I can't imagine using anything other than the best quality ingredients.

"Yeah, that's a crime punishable by death in a place like this, I tell you." Marco jokes lightheartedly, and I can't help but smile briefly at his attempt to joke around.

"I have been hearing that more of the newer chefs have been compromising quality ingredients to cut down on costs. Does that mean whoever is responsible for his death is a new chef?" I ask, trying to connect the dots.

Marco nods, "It is possible. But, if the rumors floating around are true, La Bella Tavola is one of the restaurants that has been trying to cut costs. The fact that his body was discovered there makes it even more complicated."

As I am trying to process all he is telling me, a question pops up in my head.

"Wait, so if he was fed shrimp even though everyone here knows that he is extremely allergic to them, wouldn't it be easy to know who killed him if they just figured out who the cook was?"

A grim expression appears on Marco's face. "If only it was that easy. The problem is nobody knows who cooked the meal. No one at the restaurant cooked penne or shrimp that day."

"But that doesn't make any sense. How could it have been on his plate then?" I ask, completely lost now.

"I don't know, but Lorenzo has been adamant about the fact that no one from his restaurant bought shrimp that day, so it would have been impossible for anyone to put it into Alistair's meal. The police have investigated the entire kitchen staff, and everyone has denied making it. I am sure the police thought the same thing as you, but considering there are no cameras in the kitchen, they can't do much." Marco explains with a resigned tone.

But his words flip a switch in my head, and I look at him with wide eyes. "I think I know exactly who could give us some answer," I tell him, instantly standing up.

Marco looks at me for a moment before he smiles and mumbles, "There she is."

I can't help but grin at the way he says that, but my focus shifts immediately back to the case. And this time, I am determined to find out the truth for the last time.

Chapter Five

The Bait

The market is bustling even at this hour, something of which I will never tire. I hurry down the cobblestone streets, bursting with energy and curiosity.

I finally have a new lead, one that might be strong enough to solve this entire case for the last time. I can't believe that I thought Marco wouldn't be able to help me. If I had asked for his help before, I could have solved this case much sooner than this.

Even now, as both of us make our way to Paolo, the local seafood vendor, my mind is racing with a million possibilities. The minute Marco told me the cause of Alistair's death was a reaction to shrimp, I could only think of visiting this place. We took a small break to drop Pepperoni off at my place before we were on our way.

It is well-known that there is only one vendor in the entirety of Cinque Terre that sold seafood, and that man was Paolo. Whoever bought the fish must have come here, which means Paolo can give us the answers that we have been desperately trying to find.

Marco walks beside me, casually matching my stride. Here I am, almost jogging while he and his long legs make it appear like he is taking a simple stroll through the market.

Even though he hadn't said much yet, it was clear that Marco was impressed by my deduction skills.

But it is too soon to gloat. Even though I am hoping that Paolo will be able to help me, I still don't know for sure. There is still so much that could go wrong, but for now, I keep my fingers crossed.

The market buzzes with the sounds of vendors calling out their wares, and the air is filled with the smells of meat, fish, and various vegetables. But considering that I like to buy all my ingredients myself from the market, I have become used to the smell and the bustling crowd.

Marco and I stick close as we finally near the seafood stall, spotting Paolo standing behind the counter. I take a deep breath, praying to finally solve this case and put an end to it. There is a nagging feeling inside me telling me it simply can't be that easy, but I push the thoughts away as both Marco and I come to a stop in front of Paolo's shop.

"Oh, Filomena. I wasn't expecting you today." He greets me with a look of surprise and curiosity on his weathered face.

I smile at him politely. Paolo and I have always been on good terms in all the years that I have been purchasing seafood from him. So, I hope that he will be able to help me out today.

"Yeah, this is an unplanned visit of sorts. I am not here to buy anything, but rather, I have a few questions to ask if you have time to answer them." I explain, being as straightforward as possible.

Paolo's brow furrowed at that. "Sure, of course, anything for you," he says, clearly confused.

"I am sure you remember the day that Alistair died. It's regarding that; I am afraid." I tell him, feeling weird even talking about it. Despite that Alistair was a nuisance, his death is still hard to believe.

"Alistair? That was a terrible thing, eh? How can I help?" Paolo's interest instantly heightens at the mention of the man's name. Everyone in this place is curious about what happened, and it makes sense.

A murder taking place in a reputable restaurant is not something that happens in a peaceful town like Cinque Terre.

Marco and I exchange a quick look, and he nods encouragingly, prompting me to ask Paolo the question that has been brimming inside me.

I turn to Paolo again and finally ask him the question, holding my breath as I wait for him to answer. "Do you remember who bought shrimp on the day he died?"

Surprise flickers on his face for a moment, caught off-guard at such a question. But his eyes narrow as he tries to think hard.

He takes a moment, trying to remember. Marco waits patiently, but I tap my foot incessantly, filled with trepidation over what he might say.

Finally, after a minute or so, Paolo responds, talking slowly. "Shrimp? That day, eh? I do remember... it's strange, actually. Three people bought shrimp from me. I don't usually sell so much shrimp in one day."

My heart pounds at his words. A million possibilities rush into my head, but I shove them away and focus on Paolo. "Can you remember who they were? Or what time they came?"

Paolo scratches his chin thoughtfully. "One was a young woman, a tourist, I think. She came early in the morning, just after I opened. Then, there was an older man around noon, a regular customer of mine. But the last one..." He pauses, his gaze shifting as if recalling something odd. "I am sorry; it's just been a while. My memory is getting hazy. Maybe I am confused." He says, his tone sounding his age.

But I give him a reassuring smile. "It's alright, Paolo. There is no rush; take your time to remember." I tell him politely and he nods gratefully.

"As far as I remember, there was one other person who came to the shop that day. Weird man, I must say. I don't think I have seen him around here much before, nor do I remember what he looks like now. But there is one thing about him that made him stand out." Paolo shares, making both Marco and I pause, holding our breath as we wait for him to finish his sentence.

"How so?" This time it is Marco who prompts Paolo to continue, anticipation and curiosity evident in his voice.

"The thing about him that stood out was that he came late, around the time that I was closing. It was late in the afternoon. He seemed to be in a rush for some reason, which only annoyed me more, but what is even more strange is that he seemed to be allergic to shellfish." Paolo recalls, and that makes Marco, and I straighten.

"Allergic?" Marco repeats, and Paolo nods.

"It was odd. Most customers prefer to select their own shrimp, but he asked me to bag it for him. I didn't understand why he was even at a seafood stall if he was allergic to shellfish. When I asked him, he just brushed it off, saying it was for somebody else. I didn't bother asking more. I'd had a long day already, so I just packed his fish up, and he was gone in a heartbeat. Strange man, I tell you." Paolo finishes sharing his story, and both Marco and I share a look, a spark of realization passing between us.

"Paolo, can you remember what time it was?" I ask. I just need one last confirmation to ensure that this is the man we are looking for.

Paolo thought for a moment. "It must've been just after 5 p.m. Many of the other vendors had already closed for the day."

I grin, wanting to do a victory dance. This is it; this was all we needed to know. Whoever killed Alistair is allergic to shellfish, and that is exactly what we need to expose him. I turn to Paolo again, flashing him a million-dollar smile, "Thanks, Paolo. You have been extremely helpful."

"Of course. Come back soon. We have a great batch of fish coming in this season."

I smile politely, "Will do. I have a strong feeling that my café is going to be filled with people soon enough, and I will be needing your seafood then."

He nods at me before getting back to his work.

Marco and I leave the market together, both in a hurry to find a private space to talk. As soon as we find a quiet corner, we stop there.

"This is it; it all makes sense. According to Paolo, the man bought the shrimp late in the afternoon. That fits with the timeline." I say excitedly, unable to hold back my enthusiasm.

Marco's eyes light up too, and both of us feel elated about finally getting somewhere in this case. "What if the killer was trying to cover their tracks by using the shrimp to make it look like an accident? But they forgot one thing—their own allergy," he says, with a look of mischief.

A slow smile spreads across my face as I look at Marco. "Exactly. And I think we can use that against them."

"It's surprising how you are the same woman who was on the verge of crying not long ago," he teases, the mood lightening and the familiar spark between us reigniting.

"Cut me some slack; my entire career was threatened," I say, lightly smacking his arm.

He chuckles at that. "OK now! If there is anyone here who has the right to feel offended, it's me." he quips, turning the table against me.

"And why is that?" I ask, folding my arms as I raise an eyebrow in question.

"Aren't you the one who doubted my usefulness a while ago?" he challenges, and I can't help but grin up at him guiltily.

"OK, OK. You have proven to be quite helpful today. I am sorry I assumed otherwise. But hey, now I at least know that you are more than just a pretty face, huh." It's my turn to tease him, and he seems to be enjoying the banter just as much as I am.

"And it turns out that you are a great detective with a very sharp tongue," he throws back, and I can't help but feel giddy at his flirting.

This back and forth has gone on between us for years, but I haven't had the guts to truly think much about it. For some reason, at this moment, it feels different. The playful mood dies down slowly, our expressions softening as our eyes meet.

"You did very well today, though," he says softly.

I can't help but feel my cheeks get hot from the intense way that he is looking at me. "I wouldn't have been able to do this without you, Marco," I admit, my voice low. The tension between us is charged, but there is something tender in the way he looks at me.

"I am right here, Filomena. You don't have to do this alone." His words sounded more like a promise than reassurance.

I smile up at him, believing him. He has always been there for me.

"Well, then. Let's get a plan in motion and finally expose the person responsible for this entire mess." I say, and a slow smile spreads on our faces as we both start to plan the downfall of the person who killed Alistair.

The Resolution

Chapter Six

The Festival and the Trap

The annual Harbour Festival is in full gear, with the constant buzz of laughter and conversation. Strung lights are crisscrossed over the town square, giving it a festive glow. Tantalizing smells of meat grilling and freshly baked pastries waft from booths where regional cooks are displaying their best creations.

The festival is an event the town of Cinque Terre looks forward to all year, me included. This year I will not only be highlighting my Porcini Penne with a truffle sauce, but I have an additional mission—to unfold the mystery of Alistair Fitzwilliam's. It has grappled the town with fear and confusion for long enough.

I'm hoping the new information we got from Paolo can potentially lead us somewhere. I realize multiple people can be allergic to shrimp, but I know the culprit will be consciously trying to hide their guilt. They're bound to make a mistake. Any subtle or minor blunder will expose their identity. I'll be ready for it. Hopefully, this festival is going to be the key to finding the perpetrator.

"Filomena, the competition is about to start! Are you ready?" Marco's face is twisted in anxious tension and curiosity as he approaches me.

He has been my partner in crime through all of this. Together we have brainstormed ideas on how to bait the murderer. Although he did seem skeptical at first about the effectiveness of my plans, he agreed to support me in the end. That has been all the motivation I need to take the next step.

"As ready as ever!" I shrug my shoulders.

He shakes his head chuckling.

"I never knew you could be this daring. You're more than just some flavor maestro after all. There's way more depth to you than what meets the eye," he comments as we walk together toward the booth. Feeling his eyes on me, I turn around to find him staring intently at me. I can feel the heat in his glare.

Get a hold of yourself, Filomena! You have a mission to accomplish!

I chide myself, shaking my head to clear the distracting thoughts so I can focus on the task at hand.

We arrive at the arena where the competition is being held. I squint my eyes and scan the crowd, taking in the excited faces of the onlookers who have gathered to witness the cooking competition.

"Buonasera! Today, we have gathered to participate in the decades-old Harbour Festival. Just like every year, we have brought in your favorite chefs from all over the city. This is not just some competition, but also an event where you all will get a chance to taste the creations of our talented chefs. However, here's a little twist. At the end of this competition, there will be a lucky draw, and the winners will get to taste our chefs' specialties.

The chefs can also participate in the tasting event of their competition. All the participants are required to fill out this form to state any food allergies they might suffer from. We wouldn't want our special guests to get sick, do we?" Matteo, the host, and a good friend of mine, announces with zeal. He winks at me discreetly as he signals for me to take my position.

I smirk with a curt nod. He is another one of my accomplices on this mission.

"Good luck!" Marco whispers, giving my hand a gentle squeeze.

"Thanks!" Taking a deep breath, I walk toward the small, round table where my culinary creation is already proudly displayed.

All ten chefs are dressed in crisp white aprons as they stand in front of their tables with nervous excitement and anticipation. The audience watches intently as the judges start to make rounds and listen to the chefs explain the ingredients and inspiration behind their special dishes.

At any other time, I would have been solely focused on presenting my food. But right now, all I can think about is whether the bait will be effective. I'm alert the entire time, my eyes bouncing between the team of cooks, the judges, and the audience.

I'm determined not to miss any possible lead.

Meanwhile, the judges evaluate the food and leave to discuss the winner. While they wait for the results, the participants are given time to fill in the forms. Once all the forms are complete, Matteo surreptitiously signals for me to follow him. My heart races with anticipation as we make our way backstage.

He heads to a secluded corner with Marco and me trailing closely behind. Nobody is paying attention to us; they are too caught up in the lively atmosphere.

The three of us stand in a closed circle as Matteo presents me with the forms while running his eyes around to see if someone is watching—tiny beads of sweat form on my forehead despite the crisp wind coming from the harbour. Grabbing the forms, I give half to Marco while I clutch the other half in my hand. There seems to be over a hundred in total.

"My job is done. I'm signing off now!" Matteo smiles as he gives a gentle pat on my back.

"Thanks, Matteo. I owe you for this." After giving him a tight hug, I refocus my attention on the task at hand.

"Let's get this over with!" With a nervous exhale, I start analyzing the forms. There are several food allergies mentioned, but I'm looking for a particular one: shellfish.

It takes us over ten minutes to sort through the forms. Three people have noted a shellfish allergy. Anxiously, Marco and I exchange a look. My mind races with all sorts of doubts. How can I know which one is the culprit? Was I too optimistic about the success of my plan?

"Now what?" Marco asks the question I have been dreading hearing. "We need to hurry the judges are about to announce the results."

"These names don't ring a bell. Do you know any of them?" I ask, ignoring his question.

"Um, let me see," Marco grabs the three questionnaires and scrutinizes them with a frown.

"I think I know two of them. The first one, Giulia, is a new entrepreneur in the town. She owns a boutique down the market square. The other is Alessandro, a middle-aged fisherman. I don't think they have any reason to kill Alistair," he concludes with a puzzled look on his face. "Plus, Paolo said that the suspicious customer was a male."

Pressing my lips, I stimulate my mind to think. A new boutique owner... and an unproblematic fisherman... their connection to the murder of a food critic doesn't make any sense.

That leaves only one suspect. The name "Ricky" is unfamiliar to both Marco and me. "It's Ricky," I say breathlessly, casting a nervous glance at Marco.

He nods in agreement.

I make a spur-of-the-moment decision—a decision that is either going to lead me to the culprit or a dead end.

There's no time to dwell on what is at stake.

Returning the forms to Matteo discreetly, I tell him which person I want to taste my food item. He nods and leaves to announce the result.

"So, we have conducted the drawing, and here are the results," he announces in a loud, energetic voice, eliciting an excited reaction from the participants.

I shift my weight nervously as he goes through the names one by one. My stomach somersaults when the "lucky winner" is announced. Everyone claps for the individual selected to sample my dish.

With a racing heart, I turn my head to see who the mysterious "Ricky" is. My gaze lands on a man dressed in the same crisp white uniform as me. I immediately recognize Riccardo—a young chef who opened his restaurant a few months ago—one of the chefs who had been a target of Alistair's cruel criticism.

My head starts spinning as I stare at him dumbfounded. Ricky must be a nickname which is why I didn't recognize it on his questionnaire.

He is the one who murdered Alistair.

I can't believe this is happening.

"So, now we request that our winners come on the stage to sample these dishes prepared by Cirque Terra's finest chefs," Matteo's exuberant tone is followed by the sound of applause as the winners come to the respective tables to taste the food.

I remain frozen in place, my eyes fixated on Riccardo, AKA "Ricky." He smiles while confidently gliding toward me."

"Filomena, always been a fan of your culinary skills!" He says with an excited tone as he approaches my table.

"I'm glad. Are you ready to experience a taste of heaven?" I say, arching an eyebrow. My tone holds a hidden challenge as I plaster a smile on my face. Not getting what I mean by it, he nods.

Then noticing the familiar porcini penne, Ricky's eyes grow wide as he reluctantly takes a small bite.

He looks okay at first, but then, he starts sneezing violently. I cross my arms over my chest as I glance at Marco, who is looking at the scene before him intently. I also spot Constable Ricci in the crowd. I give him a thumbs-up, and he nods before getting on the stage.

Riccardo is slouched over gasping for breath. A barely audible "shrimp..." escapes his mouth.

Constable Ricci yanks him up to a standing position.

The spectators quit chatting and chanting as soon as they notice the scene before them. Constable Ricci grabs both his arms to detain him.

"This is the man who killed Alistair," I claim as I take center stage. A collective gasp of shock escapes the crowd as they hear my accusation.

There are many confused glances thrown my way as they switch their gazes between me and Riccardo.

"We have quietly been investigating the case of Alistair's death. We discovered that the person responsible also had a shellfish allergy. To capture the murderer, I laid out bait with the help of Constable Ricci. I prepared the same dish that cost Alistair his life, knowing the murderer would recognize the sauce which contained hidden shrimp. Alistair heavily criticized Riccardo's restaurant and cuisine when he opened four months ago. All evidence points to him being the murderer," I conclude, sweeping my gaze across the crowd to see their expressions.

"She's lying!" Riccardo yells as he tries to free himself from Ricci's grip.

"Lying? Are you denying that his reviews almost shut you down? Are you denying buying shrimp on the day of the murder even though you are allergic to it? How could you go as far as murder?" I ask him with a disgusted look.

He glares at me, his eyes and nose red because of the allergic reaction, and then, with a fuming silence, he scans the crowd with the same expression until he returns his gaze to me once again. He starts shaking his head vehemently, as if he's disappointed in me for some reason. His body starts shivering, and something tells me it's out of anger. I'm truly scared to look at his eyes.

"You were also the one at the receiving end of his horrendous 'reviews'. You of all people should understand why I did it!" He hisses, trying to take a step closer but Ricci pulls him back. My heart picks up its pace. He looks furious as if he's ready to launch himself.

The other chefs have exited the stage now. It only leaves us three until Marco jumps up to come by my side, holding my hand in his in silent comfort.

"Nothing justifies you murdering someone!" I spit disgustingly. Despite being afraid of him at the moment, I stand my ground. I didn't think he would confess right away, but I believe he has a short temper and potentially some mental issues. It's good that he decided to confess. It makes closing this case a little easier to be honest.

"He tried to ruin me, and you're saying it doesn't justify the murder? He gave me bad reviews. He discovered the cheap ingredients in my food and was threatening to expose me. I would have been ruined to ashes if that happened. He was also supposed to be a judge here if he was alive. So yes, I had every justification to get rid of him," he heaves as he pauses to scowl at the crowd.

"Instead of thanking me for saving all of you from him, you set a trap for me. I can't believe this!" He sputtered with rage.

An entire crowd has gathered to witness his confession to murder. The onlookers stand in disbelief at what they are hearing.

"You're under arrest for the murder of Alistair Fitzwilliam," Ricci handcuffs him straight away and drags him down the stage toward the police car.

There's a shocking after-effect on the crowd, the dark revelation a strange contrast against the lively festival, bringing it to an abrupt halt. It doesn't matter anymore. What matters is that the culprit has been found, and he is behind bars.

Chapter Seven

Aftermath and New Beginning

"Let's go, Pepperoni!" I let out a hearty chuckle when Pepperoni stops for his usual sniffing game as we walk down the cobblestone pathway toward the beach. My partner in crime takes his sweet time to explore. It was basically because of him that I was able to discover the dead body in the first place.

The town felt relieved with Riccardo arrested. I have gained respect from the townspeople over the success of the investigation. I smile awkwardly in response to their comments, reminiscing back to my favorite childhood pastime of solving puzzles.

The town gathered to celebrate Riccardo's arrest and for the announcement of the competition's winner—the one and only, Filomena Rossi!

With the murder solved and tourist season in full swing, I can now devote my attention to La Nonna's Nonna.

"Hey, Filomena! What are you up to?" Chiara waves at me from the other end of the street. Smiling, I wave back. She is a regular at La Nonna's Nonna.

"Just heading down to Monterosso al Mare. It's a quiet sunny day, perfect for the beach. Isn't it?" I yell across the street as I inform her of my plans. I'm feeling quite chirpy this morning.

"Indeed. Have fun!" She yells before jogging down the street in her sleek black leather boots. I smile at her knack for striking fashion.

We walk for a few more minutes until the familiar picturesque view is in sight. I take a moment to appreciate the tranquility and natural charm of the beach. It has been so long since I came here last. I appreciate Marco's suggestion that we meet at the beach and take a well-deserved break.

I smile as I make my way down the hill toward the shore. I can already smell the salty aroma of the ocean and the sand. My eyes scan the beachgoers until they land on a familiar figure, lounging in a chair under an umbrella. He waves as he sees me approaching.

"Marco!" I greet him enthusiastically. He sits up straight in his lounge chair and pulls up his shades.

"You look wonderful!" He smiles, his gaze traveling up and down. I squirm under the intensity of his watchful eyes. I'm dressed in a sheer white shirt and shorts with a bikini underneath. I don't know what's so wonderful about my outfit, but he clearly appreciates it.

Or he just wants to flirt with you! My mind swirls.

"Thank you. It's such a peaceful day!" I comment with a content sigh as I sit and close my eyes, breathing in the crisp breeze of the sea.

"It is. I'm glad that you accepted my offer to join me and abandon your precious restaurant for a day," he says with a chuckle.

"Maria is there to take care of the restaurant. Besides, we don't have that many customers in the morning. So, I thought why not? I deserve a break after all!" I shrug, tying Pepperoni's leash to my lounge chair so he can't sprint towards the waves.

He barks excitedly as he watches the children play with the ball. I make a mental note to play with him later.

"You truly do. The Riccardo mystery was a hectic one to solve. I'm still amazed at how things unfolded. At first, when you suggested laying out the trap, I was a bit skeptical. However, I've decided you have quite the talent for cracking mysteries. You should have been a detective!" He chuckles, his tone half joking and half serious.

My lips stretch into an amused smile as I shake my head, "Believe it or not, I did consider that when I was young, but I was more interested in cooking. That is my passion. Always has been. Solving mysteries is just a hobby," I inform him leaning back against the chair as the warm sunlight envelops my body.

Feeling too dressed for the purpose, I sit up straight and pull off my shirt. Next, come my shorts. The only piece of clothing now covering my body is my yellow bikini.

I can feel Marco's eyes on me, but I try to ignore it. Still, my heartbeat increases a little at the attention I'm receiving.

"How do you feel about being named the big winner? I didn't even get the chance to congratulate you on your achievement!" He says, finally leaning against the chair and turning his body toward me.

"It feels like a dream. This time, I didn't even put much effort into the dish I prepared because my mind was occupied with solving the murder. I also thought about the possibility that the judges might eliminate me because I included an ingredient in my recipe that I kept hidden from everyone. Of course, I couldn't reveal the shellfish sauce because it would've ruined our plan. But I still won. I feel like it's the reward for my hard work, not for preparing the dish but for exposing the culprit. You know what I mean?"

"And I want to thank you, Marco. I wouldn't have been successful in this if it weren't for your support and cooperation. You were with me every step of the plan. Thank you." Letting out a sigh, I smile at him, showing how grateful I am for his presence by my side.

His face lights up as he returns my smile.

"It's the least I could do after all you did for this town. You are a brave lady, Filomena!" He says appreciatively, placing his hand on top of mine.

Just a little touch is enough to send my heart into a frenzy. I stare up into his eyes as we're both lying down on the chairs, with his hands on top of mine. He also looks taken aback at the sudden proximity but doesn't pull back his hands.

"Tell me something about yourself," I ask when I find him staring for too long. His gaze always makes me feel giddy. He seems to come out of the trance as he pulls his hand away.

"What do you want to know?" He asks, a pleasant smile plastered on his face.

"Tell me about your childhood or your family. Now that I think about it, I realize there's not much I know about you. I feel like you're such a mystery. And you know about my knack for solving mysteries, right?" I tell him light-heartedly, chuckling at the end.

His body visibly stiffens as he shifts uncomfortably in his seat. He avoids looking into my eyes and sits up straight. I feel like I have said something wrong. Is it unusual to ask about family or childhood to someone who's been your partner in crime and with whom you feel this unexplainable spark?

Truthfully, I don't know much about him. He has never shared anything about himself. I didn't ask either because as we were getting closer, I was too focused on the murder. Now that it all has passed, I can ask him anything I want to know.

Or that's what I thought!

I thought that under the warm glow of the sun, we would talk and share our dreams, but nothing of that sort happened. The peaceful morning turns tense as Marco stands up and puts on his shirt and pants.

"What's wrong, Marco?" I ask, standing up as well with a frown on my face. I don't know what I said that offended him so much that he is ready to leave without any explanation! I feel frustrated to no end.

"I think I have some important matters to deal with at the restaurant. I'm sorry to leave this abruptly, but we'll plan to do this again some other day, OK?" The smile doesn't reach his eyes as he takes off, leaving me bewildered and exasperated.

I know that the question must have irritated him, but why?

Even if it did, he should have at least told me. I would have understood. I didn't appreciate how he left me hanging like this.

Anyway, nothing can be done. He left and spoiled my mood.

"We're going back to La Nonna's Nonna!" I tell Pepperoni with an infuriated sigh. He barks as he sees me taking him off the beach without letting him play, but I can't do anything. The day is spoiled, and I need to leave.

The whole way to the restaurant, my mind swirls with different scenarios of why he must have behaved that way. I don't know anything about his past, and maybe there are things he's uncomfortable sharing...

Anyway, he'll share when he wants. I won't force him. I'm just bothered by him abruptly leaving me when meeting at the beach had been his idea in the first place.

"Maria, I'm back!" I announce as soon as I enter the restaurant.

"Huh? Didn't you say you'll be back in the afternoon?" She tilts her head outside of the kitchen with a perplexed expression.

"I did, but something came up, so I'm here. Anyway, did any customers come?" I ask, taking a seat on one of the vintage chairs.

"Yeah. Just a few, but I managed them. Oh, and you received a box. I haven't checked it. Maybe, some love interest has sent you a little something?" She wiggles her eyebrows playfully. I shrug with a dismissive wave. Other times, I would have fired back and joined her in her teasing, but not now. I'm not in the mood. Thanks to Marco!

"Let's see what it is!" I grab the box that's neatly wrapped in black paper. Frowning, I open the mystery box, and it contains nothing but a piece of paper.

Unfolding the paper, my hands freeze, and my eyes widen as I read the words out loud.

You thought you could win at life by winning a mere competition, huh? Let's see how far your hotheadedness can take you! The bad days are coming. Please look forward to it!

The Deep Dive

Chapter Eight

The Rival Chef

The sun's still low in the sky when I open La Nonna's Nonna for the day. The scent of the sea rolls in through the half-cracked windows, mingling with the smell of garlic from the night before. I stand at the front of the restaurant, looking out over the quiet harbour of Cinque Terre.

Boats bob gently in the distance, their shadows stretching long over the water, but my mind isn't on the view. My thoughts flood with the memory of Alistair Fitzwilliam sprawled on La Bella Tavola's floor, his twisted, sneering face haunting my every waking moment.

The townspeople are relieved after Riccardo's arrest; even Lorenzo came to me the other day thanking me for the help.

"But who could have sent that note?" I mutter under my breath.

Pepperoni, my ever-loyal beagle, sniffs at my feet, wagging his tail in response to my rhetorical question. He's the only one who's really helping me in this mess. The police—well, they've been thorough in their usual halfhearted way.

Constable Ricci is more interested in what's on today's menu than in finding any real closure. That leaves me with one option: I may have to figure this note out myself.

Recalling the note and the fact that the sender mentioned the competition, I think of people, especially those with eatery businesses, who might have a grudge against me. I think of all the chefs and owners I know, but one name stands out: Giovanna Baldini.

Giovanna. Even her name makes my lips curl.

I walk over to the counter and grab my notebook, flipping through my scribbled thoughts. Giovanna has had it in for me since the moment I opened La Nonna's Nonna. Her restaurant, Il Paradiso del Mare, is just down the street. For years, it was the spot for tourists and locals alike. But as soon as I showed up with my fettuccine gorgonzola and limoncello tiramisù, her customer base started to shrink. That alone wouldn't be enough to make her a suspect but hearing that she didn't participate in the event because of me kind of makes her one.

I glance down at Pepperoni, who is looking up at me expectantly.

"Come on, boy. We're going to pay a visit to Giovanna."

***

The streets of Cinque Terre are narrow and winding, like some labyrinth designed to confuse the uninitiated. But I've lived here long enough to navigate them with ease. Il Paradiso del Mare is tucked away between two pastel-colored buildings, its elegant signage swinging lazily in the soft morning breeze. The restaurant is quiet, the kitchen staff not yet bustling with their usual fervor. Good. I want Giovanna before the day's chaos begins.

Pepperoni and I push through the heavy wooden door, the faint jingle of the bell above us echoing through the empty dining room. The scent of fresh herbs hits me immediately—basil, rosemary, oregano. It's a sharp contrast to the saltiness of the sea air just outside.

"Filomena." Her voice is as cold as the chilled prosecco she serves on summer afternoons. I turn, and there she is—Giovanna Baldini, standing behind the counter with her arms crossed and her dark hair pulled back so tightly I wonder how her head isn't throbbing. She looks me up and down, her eyes narrowing when they land on Pepperoni, who is busy sniffing around the legs of a nearby chair.

"Giovanna," I say, forcing a smile that isn't shared with my heart. "I'm here to check on you."

She raises an eyebrow. "Why?"

I lean against the counter, trying to seem casual, but I can feel the tension crackling between us like electricity. "Is it true that you refused to participate because of me?"

Her expression doesn't change, but I see the slight tightening of her jaw. She knows what I'm here for.

"Oh, so you think you're that important?" Her voice is like honey-coated steel—sweet but with an edge that could cut if you're not careful.

I shrug, feigning nonchalance. "I heard you had a bit of an argument with the organizers and even pulled out your name at the last moment. I figured I'd come by and get your side of the story."

Giovanna scoffs, turning away from me to grab a towel and wipe down the already spotless counter. "Everyone in this town is free to choose what they want. I didn't want to compete because I had other things to do. I don't have time to worry about all this little stuff."

I chuckle sarcastically and decide to push further. "I suppose that's true. I thought you might like to know that I received a threatening note yesterday, a note saying I should stay out of it. I wonder what would happen if I dug more into it. After all, Alistair's murder is still pretty fresh in people's minds. Just guessing that if something were to happen to me, well... let's just say that it probably would look suspicious." I keep my tone casual yet drop subtle hints.

Her hand stops mid-wipe. She's frozen, just for a moment, before she tosses the towel aside and faces me again.

"So what? Alistair was murdered because of his shitty attitude," she snaps. "That man had no respect for the art of cooking. He thought he could waltz in here and judge years of challenging work with a single bite. Yes, I told him off. I told him that if he ever set foot in Il Paradiso del Mare again, he'd regret it. But I didn't kill him, Filomena. You, on the other hand, should be careful since you're the one being threatened apparently."

I tilt my head, studying her face. She's angry, sure, but there's something else there—something raw and unguarded. Desperation, maybe? Fear? I can't quite tell.

"Why should I believe you?" I ask quietly.

Giovanna's eyes flash, and for a moment, I think she's going to lunge across the counter. Instead, she takes a deep breath and lets it out slowly. "Because as much as I hated him, I wouldn't throw my life away over one lousy review. You, of all people, should understand that."

I don't say anything, but I can feel my resolve wavering. She's right. Alistair was a tyrant, but would she really kill him over a review? I chew on my lip, thinking it over.

"Fine," I say at last. "But if I find out you were behind..."

She cuts me off, her voice dripping with sarcasm. "You'll what? Sic your dog on me?"

Pepperoni perks up at the mention of his name, his tail wagging as if he's actually considering it.

I sigh and turn to leave, but as I reach the door, something catches my eye. A small, crumpled piece of paper is on the floor near the counter. I bend down to pick it up, smoothing it out with my fingers. It's a receipt for a delivery, but not just any delivery—shrimp. Lots of it.

"Shrimp, huh?" I ask, holding up the receipt. "I thought you only used local seafood."

Giovanna's face pales, just for a second, but then she recovers. "It's for a special event," she says quickly. "A one-time thing. And stop tying it with Alistair's murder. You've already bagged the fame by capturing Riccardo. That boat has sailed, so leave me and my business out of it."

I nod slowly, slipping the receipt into my pocket. "Right. A one-time thing. Well, thanks for your time, Giovanna. I'll see you around."

As Pepperoni and I step out into the sunlight, I can feel her eyes burning into my back. I don't believe her. Not for a second. But that's not enough to go on. Not yet anyway.

Back at La Nonna's Nonna, the lunchtime rush is just beginning. The clatter of dishes and the hum of conversation fill the air, but my mind is elsewhere. I'm standing at the counter, staring at the receipt I took from Giovanna's restaurant. Shellfish. It seems so innocent, but something about it doesn't sit right with me. I pull out my notebook and jot down a quick note: *shrimp delivery—Giovanna lying? Connection to Alistair?*

Just as I'm about to tuck the notebook away, the door swings open, and in walks Enzo, my busboy. He's young, barely out of school, with wild dark hair that refuses to be tamed no matter how much he tries. He greets me with a half-hearted smile. There's something off about him today.

"You OK, Enzo?" I ask, watching as he grabs a broom and starts sweeping the floor with more aggression than necessary.

He shrugs, avoiding my gaze. "Fine. Just... tired."

"Uh-huh." I walk over to him, leaning against the counter. "You've been working here long enough for me to know when something's bothering you. Spill."

He stops sweeping and looks at me, his expression conflicted. For a moment, I think he's going to brush me off again, but then he sighs heavily and leans on the broom handle.

"It's about... well, it's about Alistair."

My ears perk up. "What about him?"

Enzo hesitates, glancing around the room as if he's worried someone might overhear. "I didn't want to say anything before, but... I saw something."

I frown, my pulse quickening. "Saw what?"

He swallows hard. "The night of Alistair's murder there was a delivery near La Bella Tavola. It didn't make sense because it was so late. Anyway, I didn't think much of it at the time, but now... now I'm not so sure. But I wasn't able to see the delivery person's face."

My mind races. A late-night delivery? My mind goes back to the shrimp receipt that I found at Giovanna's. I lean in closer, trying to keep my voice calm. "Did you see what he delivered?"

Enzo shakes his head. "No, but it was a big box. Heavy-looking. And he seemed... nervous. Like he didn't want anyone to see him."

I feel a cold shiver run down my spine. This could be the lead I've been waiting for.

"Enzo, if you remember anything else—anything at all—you come straight to me, OK?"

He nods, looking relieved. "Yeah, I will. Thanks, Filomena."

As Enzo goes back to sweeping, I head to the kitchen, my heart pounding in my chest. The pieces are starting to come together, but there's still something missing. Something crucial.

I need to find that delivery man.

***

Later that afternoon, once the lunch rush has died down, I decide to visit the town's resident delivery guy. If anyone knows about late-night deliveries in Cinque Terre, it's him. His small, cluttered office tucked away behind the fish market, and the smell of brine and seaweed hits me like a wall as I approach.

Pepperoni and I step inside, and Louis looks up from his desk, squinting at us through his thick glasses.

"Ah, Filomena," he says, leaning back in his chair. "What brings you here?"

I waste no time, cutting straight to the point. "I need to know about a delivery. Late at night, after hours. A big box. Heavy. Ring any bells?"

Louis scratches his chin, his brow furrowing. "Late-night delivery, huh? Not many of those around here. Why do you need to know?"

"It might have been linked to Alistair Fitzwilliam's murder."

His eyes widen slightly, and I can see the wheels turning in his head. He shifts uncomfortably in his seat.

"Look, Filomena, I don't want any trouble, OK? Also, hasn't the guy already been caught? Why are you digging into it anyway?"

I narrow my eyes. "Trouble? I'm not here to cause trouble, Louis. I just need answers."

He sighs, rubbing the back of his neck. "Alright, alright. There was a delivery. Late at night, like you said. But it wasn't me who made it. There's this guy—who came in only a year or so ago and took over some of my late shifts. He's quiet and keeps to himself. Name's Luca."

I jot the name down in my notebook. "Luca. Where can I find him?"

Louis shrugs. "He's hard to pin down. Moves around a lot. But I hear he hangs out at the marina sometimes, near the old warehouse. Might be worth checking out. But be careful Filomena. I've heard that he might be connected to the local mafia."

I thank Louis and head for the door, my mind buzzing with new possibilities. As Pepperoni and I make our way toward the marina, I can't shake the feeling that we're getting closer. Closer to the truth.

Standing on the dock, I gaze out at the sea. The sun is sinking low, casting a golden glow over the water, but my thoughts are dark. If Luca had something to do with that late-night delivery, then I'm one step closer to solving this mystery. But there's still so much I don't know.

Pepperoni sits by my side, his nose twitching as the salty breeze ruffles his fur. He looks up at me, his eyes wide and expectant.

I crouch down, giving him a gentle pat on the head.

"We're getting closer, boy," I whisper. "We'll find out the truth. I promise."

As the last light of day fades and the shadows of the harbor stretch longer across the cobblestones, I know one thing for certain—whoever Luca is, he holds the key to unlocking this puzzle. And I'm not stopping until I find him.

Chapter Nine

The Local Mafia

The morning fog clings to the stone walls of Cinque Terre as I step out of La Nonna's Nonna. The narrow streets are quieter than usual, the soft sound of waves crashing against the rocky shore echoing through the empty alleyways.

The air is thick with the scent of saltwater and fresh-baked bread from the bakery down the street, but my mind is too preoccupied to appreciate the usual charm of my seaside town.

After yesterday's conversation with Louis, I feel like I'm finally closing in on something important. The name "Luca" keeps rattling around in my head, raising more questions than answers.

Late-night deliveries, nervous glances, and that heavy box... it all feels like pieces of a puzzle, but I'm still not sure how they fit together. Pepperoni trots beside me, nose to the ground, searching for clues in his own way.

I tighten my grip on his leash as we walk toward the marina. I don't know what I expect to find there, but I can't shake the feeling that something bigger is brewing beneath the surface. Something darker than just a negative review or a jealous competitor.

Louis mentioned Luca, but he also hinted at something else—rumors of a local mafia presence. The thought makes my stomach churn. The mafia? Here in Cinque Terre? It seems far-fetched, but then again, every small town has its secrets.

As we approach the marina, the scent of diesel fuel mixes with the briny sea air. Fishing boats are moored along the docks, their ropes creaking as they sway gently with the rhythm of the water.

Fishermen unload crates of fresh catch, their voices low and gruff as they joke and shout orders at each other. I scan the scene, looking for any sign of Luca or anyone who might know something about him.

I approach a group of dockworkers, their hands busy sorting through nets and crates. One of them, a burly man with a thick beard and weathered skin, looks up as I get closer. His eyes narrow slightly, but he doesn't say anything.

"Excuse me," I say, trying to sound casual despite the tension twisting in my gut. "I'm looking for someone named Luca. He works as a delivery driver around town."

The man glances at his colleagues and then spits into the water before turning his gaze back to me. "Luca, huh? Why you asking?"

There's something about his tone that sets me on edge. It's not curiosity—it's caution. Maybe even fear. I swallow, keeping my voice steady. "I've heard he might know something about a delivery that was made about when Alistair Fitzwilliam was killed. I just want to ask him a few questions."

The man chuckles darkly, shaking his head. "You don't want to get mixed up with Luca, lady. Trust me on that."

"I'm already mixed up in it," I say firmly, crossing my arms. "So, where can I find him?"

For a moment, there's silence. The dockworkers exchange glances, the tension in the air thickening. Finally, the bearded man sighs and points toward an old warehouse at the far end of the dock, half-hidden in the morning mist. "Try there. But if you're smart, you'll forget you ever asked."

I nod, giving him a tight smile. "Thanks for the advice. I'll keep it in mind."

***

The warehouse looms ahead, its rusted metal doors groaning as the wind presses against them. The whole place feels forgotten, like it hasn't seen much use in years. Weeds grow up between the cracks in the pavement, and the smell of decaying fish lingers in the air, mixing with the musty scent of damp wood.

I glance down at Pepperoni, who's sniffing the ground with more enthusiasm than I feel. "Stay close, boy," I mutter, my nerves prickling. Something about this place feels... wrong.

As we approach the door, I hesitate for a moment, my hand hovering over the handle. What am I walking into? Luca isn't just some random delivery guy. There's something more to him—something dangerous. But if he's connected to Alistair's death or even the note I received, I need to know. With a deep breath, I push open the door.

Inside, the warehouse is dimly lit, the only light filtering through broken windows high above. Stacks of old crates and barrels are piled haphazardly around the space, casting long shadows across the floor. The air is thick and damp, heavy with the scent of mildew and something metallic I can't quite place.

I take a few cautious steps inside, my heart pounding in my chest. "Luca?" I call out, my voice echoing off the walls. "Luca, are you here?"

For a moment, there's no response. Just the sound of dripping water somewhere in the distance and the soft creak of wood settling in the humid air. But then, from behind a stack of crates, I hear a muffled voice.

"You should've stayed away, Filomena."

I freeze, my hand instinctively tightening on Pepperoni's leash. The voice is familiar—too familiar. Slowly, a figure steps out from the shadows. Luca. Tall, wiry, with dark eyes that glint in the low light. There's a smirk on his face, but his posture is tense like he's ready for a fight.

He is the same delivery guy I chased in the alley. My head is spinning.

"I've been looking for you," I say, trying to keep my voice steady. "I have some questions."

"I know," Luca replies, his voice cold. "And that's the problem."

Before I can react, I hear footsteps behind me—heavy, deliberate. My stomach drops as I turn to see two more men step into the warehouse, blocking the door. They're both broad-shouldered, their faces hard and expressionless. One of them cracks his knuckles, the sound echoing through the cavernous space.

My heart races. I've walked into a trap.

"You're asking too many questions, Filomena," Luca continues, taking a step closer. "This isn't your business. Alistair... he got what was coming to him. But if you keep digging, you might end up just like him."

My throat tightens, but I force myself to meet his gaze. "So, you did kill him?"

Luca's smirk falters for a moment, but he doesn't answer. Instead, he takes another step forward, his eyes flicking to the men behind me.

"It wasn't supposed to go this far. But now you're involved, and that complicates things."

"But Riccardo confessed." I look at him, still dumbfounded.

"He had to because he was tasked to."

I glance around, looking for a way out. The warehouse is large, but there's no clear exit other than the door blocked by Luca's goons. Pepperoni growls softly beside me, sensing the danger.

"I didn't want to hurt you," Luca says, his voice low and almost regretful. "But you've left me no choice."

Suddenly, everything snaps into focus. Luca isn't just some delivery driver. He's part of something bigger—something darker. The local mafia that Louis mentioned... they're real. And Luca's involved.

My mind races as I try to figure out what to do. I can't fight these men—not physically, at least. But I have to think fast. I can't let them silence me like they silenced Alistair.

"You think you're the only one who knows the truth about Alistair's death?" I say, my voice sharper now. "You're wrong."

Luca's eyes narrow. "What are you talking about?"

"I'm not the only one investigating his death. People are watching, Luca. They're asking questions. If anything happens to me, it won't go unnoticed."

It's a bluff and a shaky one at that, but I see a flicker of doubt in Luca's eyes. He hesitates, glancing back at the men behind me. For a moment, the tension in the air thickens, and I hold my breath, waiting to see if he'll take the bait.

Finally, Luca lets out a low curse, rubbing a hand over his face. "You should've stayed out of this," he mutters.

"I didn't have a choice," I say, my voice steadier now. "Just like you didn't have a choice with Alistair, right?"

Luca's jaw tightens, and for the first time, I see something in his eyes that I hadn't expected. Guilt.

Regret.

He isn't a cold-blooded killer. He's trapped, just like me.

"Look," I say, softening my tone. "I know this isn't your idea. I know you're not the one pulling the strings here. But if you help me—if you tell me who's really behind this—we can both get out of this mess."

Luca stares at me, his expression hard to read. For a long moment, there's silence. Then, finally, he sighs and takes a step back, motioning for the men to stand down.

"You don't know what you're asking for, Filomena," he says, his voice tired. "These people... they don't forgive. If I talk, I'm dead."

"And if you don't talk, we're both dead," I reply, my heart pounding in my chest. "Help me stop this."

Luca hesitates again, but then he nods—just once. "Fine. But you didn't hear this from me, understand?"

"Understood," I say quickly.

He glances around the warehouse as if checking to make sure no one else is listening, then leans in closer. "It's not just about Alistair. He wasn't just writing bad reviews. He was extorting people—powerful people. He had dirt on everyone in this town. That's why they wanted him dead."

"Who?" I whisper. "Who wanted him dead?"

Luca's eyes dart to the door, then back to me. "The Ferraro family. They run everything in this town—restaurants, deliveries, protection rackets, you name it. Alistair found out they were laundering money through the top restaurants in Cinque Terre. He was going to expose them, so they had him silenced."

My blood runs cold. The Ferraro family. I've heard the name before—whispers in the shadows, rumors in the market. They're the real power behind the scenes, the local mafia that controls everything from the food supply to the money flowing through the town.

"And now they know you're asking questions," Luca adds, his voice grim. "If they find out what you know…"

He doesn't need to finish the sentence. I know exactly what he's implying. I'm in deep—deeper than I ever imagined.

"Is there any way to stop them?" I ask, desperation creeping into my voice.

Luca shakes his head. "You don't stop the Ferraros. You just survive them."

Before I can respond, I hear a sudden noise—a loud crash from the back of the warehouse. Luca's eyes widen in panic, and he shoves me toward the door. "Go! Now! They're coming!"

I don't need to be told twice. I grab Pepperoni and bolt for the exit, my heart pounding in my chest. Behind me, I hear shouts and footsteps—whoever's coming, they're not here for a friendly chat.

We burst out of the warehouse and into the fresh air, the fog still clinging to the streets like a ghost. I don't stop running until we're halfway back to La Nonna's Nonna, my lungs burning and my legs aching. Pepperoni trots beside me, panting but determined.

As I catch my breath, I glance over my shoulder, half-expecting to see Luca's pursuers following me. But the streets are empty.

For now.

Back at the restaurant, I lock the door behind me and sink into a chair, my mind racing. The Ferraro family. Luca's warning echoes in my ears, sending a chill down my spine. I've stumbled onto something much bigger than I anticipated—something that could get me killed if I'm not careful.

I glance down at Pepperoni, who's sitting at my feet, his eyes wide and curious. "Well, boy," I mutter, running a hand through my hair. "Looks like we've got ourselves in a real mess this time."

Pepperoni lets out a soft whine, his tail wagging uncertainly. I chuckle despite myself, reaching down to scratch behind his ears.

"We'll figure this out," I say, more to myself than to him. "We have to."

But even as I say the words, I can't shake the feeling that the walls are closing in. The Ferraro family knows I'm digging. And if they're willing to kill Alistair to protect their secrets, what's to stop them from coming after me next?

I glance out the window and watch as the fog begins to lift, revealing the bustling harbor beyond. I've uncovered a dangerous truth. Now the question is: How long can I survive it?

Chapter Ten

The Wealthy Tourist

The next morning, Cinque Terre wakes beneath a bright, cloudless sky, the golden sunlight reflecting off the crystal-clear water of the harbour. It's one of those postcard-perfect days, the kind that makes me almost forget the storm brewing beneath the surface. Almost.

I sip my espresso at a small table outside La Nonna's Nonna, watching tourists wander by and fishermen haul in their catch, oblivious to the danger lurking in our quiet small town.

Pepperoni lies at my feet, lazily chewing on the corner of a napkin that somehow escaped my attention. His tail flicks back and forth in a steady rhythm, a constant reminder that, despite everything, life keeps moving.

But I can't relax, not after what happened yesterday.

The Ferraro family. The name still sends shivers down my spine. I barely escaped the warehouse after Luca's warning, and now I know for certain that Alistair's murder isn't just about food or bad reviews.

It's about something far more sinister—money laundering, blackmail, organized crime. And I've wandered straight into the middle of it.

As if on cue, I notice something out of the corner of my eye—a folded piece of paper sitting on the table next to my espresso cup. I didn't see anyone approach, yet here it is. My heart sinks. This isn't a coincidence.

I glance around, trying to spot who might have left it, but the square is bustling with tourists and locals alike, everyone going about their business. Whoever delivered the note did it quietly, anonymously, just like the last time.

With a sigh, I unfold the paper, my pulse quickening as I read the familiar scrawl.

Stop digging. This is your last warning.

No signature. No name. Just the same cold, impersonal message as before. My hand trembles slightly as I crumple the note in my fist, feeling the weight of the threat behind the words. The Ferraro family knows I'm getting closer to the truth, and they're not going to let me keep poking around without consequences.

I've never been good at taking warnings seriously.

I shove the note into my apron pocket and take a deep breath, trying to steady my nerves. I need to think. If the Ferraros are involved in Alistair's death—and it's clear now that they are—then I need to figure out who within their circle had the most to lose from his blackmail. Someone who would benefit from silencing him permanently. Luca's warning still echoes in my ears: *"You don't stop the Ferraros. You just survive them."*

But I'm not about to back down now.

"Filomena," a voice calls from behind me, breaking my concentration. I turn to see Marco standing in the doorway of his wine bar, his usual charming smile tempered by a hint of concern. He's holding a tray with two glasses of wine—Chianti, if I had to guess—and he nods toward the empty chair across from me.

"Mind if I join you?"

I offer him a small smile, though my mind is still racing. "Sure, why not? I could use the company."

Marco sets the glasses down and takes a seat, his eyes searching mine. I can tell he knows something's wrong, but he doesn't press. Instead, he hands me one of the glasses and raises his own.

"To a beautiful day in Cinque Terre," he says, his voice light and playful, though I can sense the tension beneath it.

I clink my glass against his, though the wine tastes bitter on my tongue. "A beautiful day," I murmur, though my thoughts are a thousand miles away.

We sit in silence for a moment, the noise of the town swirling around us, but Marco's gaze never leaves me. Finally, he leans forward, his voice dropping to a low murmur.

"I heard about Luca," he says quietly. "And the Ferraros."

I raise an eyebrow, surprised by how much he already knows. "Word travels fast around here."

He chuckles softly. "It always does. Especially when it comes to them."

I take a sip of my wine, letting the familiar warmth wash over me. "I'm not giving up, Marco. I can't."

He nods, his expression serious. "I know. But you need to be careful, Filomena. The Ferraros... they don't play by the rules. And they don't forgive."

"I'm starting to realize that" I mutter, glancing down at the crumpled note in my pocket. "But I'm not stopping. Someone in this town knows more than they're letting on, and I'm going to find out who."

Marco reaches across the table and takes my hand, his touch warm and reassuring. "Just promise me you'll be careful. I don't want to see you get hurt."

For a moment, the tension between us softens, and I can feel the weight of his concern. But before I can respond, a figure catches my eye, walking toward the square with a purposeful stride.

A new tourist.

The man in front of us, clad in a crisp, expensive suit, sticks out like a sore thumb. Cinque Terre isn't a town where people wear suits and roam around looking important. No, people here like comfort, they like wearing loose linens and casual clothes instead of custom-tailored suits. There is something intriguing about the man that has my eyes glued on him.

"Do you know that man?" I ask Marco, nodding at the strange man outside.

Marco turns to look at him, and I know that he is thinking the same thing as me. It's obvious this man is no tourist. His persona exudes wealth and power, the kind of person who can't be bothered to fit in anywhere.

"I can't say I do," Marco murmurs, his voice low as he keeps watching the man with narrowed eyes.

We watch as he stops right in the middle of the square, pulling out dark sunglasses as he scans his surroundings.

"Why am I getting the heebie-jeebies from this man?" I muse quietly, and despite the tension, a chuckle escapes Marco.

"Only you would use the term 'heebie-jeebies,' Filomena," he says, shaking his head with amusement evident in his tone.

I can't help the small smile that tugs at my lips, but then I look out again, remembering to keep an eye on the man in front of us.

Marco follows my gaze, "He doesn't look like the usual type of tourist we get around here."

"No," I agree. "He doesn't."

There is something calculated in the way he moves like he isn't here to admire the sights or sip limoncello by the water. But as I get a clearer look at him, I notice something familiar about his face. Alarm bells ring in my head at the familiarity, and I get even more alert.

The man disappears suddenly, lost in the crowd of other tourists, and I can't shake the wave of unease that is gnawing at me. Something about this man just doesn't sit right with me, and I can't just sit here doing nothing.

"I can hear the wheels in your head turning from here," Marco says quietly.

I look up at him, surprised at how well he can read me. "I think I've seen him before," I admit slowly, my voice low. "At the Ferraros' warehouse."

I feel him stiffen beside me, "You think he's connected?"

I nod slowly, turning to look at him. "I don't believe in such coincidences. It's pretty suspicious that he just showed up here. Not to mention that he is giving me the creeps."

On cue, I hear Pepperoni let out a soft growl, noticing the tension in the room. He is an amazingly smart dog.

But it's Marco's concerned expression that makes me a little alert and taken aback.

"I know you are hell-bent on solving this case on your own, but if that man has anything to do with the Ferraros, you need to keep your distance. It isn't wise to interfere with someone like him," he tells me, his tone dark and serious.

His eyes are intense as they meet mine, and I am at a loss for words. Although Marco and I have been friends for a long time, that line has been blurring recently.

I know that he cares for me, but his mysterious past makes everything more complicated. Despite how well we get along, it bothers me how little I know about him.

"I told you, Marco. I can't just sit back and do nothing. Whoever this man is, he is here for a reason, and I am going to find out what it is." I tell him firmly.

He sighs, his expression filled with resignation as he recognizes the determination in my voice. He knows me well enough to know that I am not going to give up.

"I get that you're trying to help, Filomena. But sometimes—" he starts. But I shake my head, not willing to listen to anything.

"I can't stop now," I cut him off, my voice firmer than I intended. "If I back down... if I let them scare me off, then what was all of this for? Alistair deserves justice, and this town deserves to know the truth."

Marco looks at me, his jaw clenched. He doesn't argue, but the frustration is clear in his eyes. After a moment, he lets out a slow breath and nods. "Just... be careful."

I give him a small, reassuring smile, "I will."

He nods back, but I can tell that he isn't convinced. The truth is that I am not either. This town is hiding a dark secret, one that is starting to cost people their lives.

And now, it is my job to make sure the secrets unravel, and the truth comes out.

Secrets and Connections

Chapter Eleven

The Town's History

For the next few days, I lay low focusing on being more observant and less impulsive. After what happened at the warehouse, I have learned my lesson and know better than to jump into situations without thinking.

This matter isn't simple. It's probably the most dangerous case I have ever worked on, with layers that keep appearing. I must keep my ears and eyes open and be intentional about my next move.

Because this time around, a single wrong move will cost me my life.

As laid back as I sounded when I was talking to Marco, it's not how I actually feel. I know just how risky this business is, and even though I am scared, I know I can't give up.

So, for the past few days, I have been keeping an eye on the mysterious man. He would often disappear while I was trying to trail him.

It took me a while to finally figure out where he was going, to the same restaurant each night. At first, I truly doubted my suspicion, considering the option that I was being too paranoid.

But I know better than to ignore my instincts. My gut feelings and intuitions have never failed me before, and they haven't failed me this time, either.

The first two nights that he visited Lorenzo's restaurant, I assumed that the man was nothing more than a privileged, arrogant person who thought he had a right to judge everyone and everything.

I listened to him as he insulted the waiters and the food, complaining about the service and the quality of the food. Although that was enough to get on my bad side, I still gave the man the benefit of the doubt.

I left before him those nights, thinking that I was being paranoid and that he only wanted to boss people around. But tonight, I am realizing the mistake I had made in not trusting my gut.

Today, instead of dining at Lorenzo's and keeping an eye on him, I decided to stay hidden in the corner where the restroom was. Something inside me kept nagging at me to stay, even after several hours passed.

That's when my suspicion heightened. Despite having come early, the man happened to stay at the restaurant even after everyone else had left, leaving the restaurant empty except for him and me.

I quietly watched him as he started to move towards the private dining area, secluded for people who make reservations. I knew immediately that something was up.

I followed him as silently as possible, pressing up against the wall and straining my ears to hear what was going on inside. One of the voices made the hair on my neck stand and my pulse quicken.

Lorenzo.

Now, here I am, standing in the restaurant where this whole series of crimes started. I can hear the stranger's infuriated voice arguing with Lorenzo.

"We had a deal," Lorenzo growls, the agitation in his voice obvious.

"Yes, we did. But these prices are too high," the elusive stranger grits out. "You had a deal with us, and you are going against it. These are not the prices we agreed on. Your greediness will cost us everything," he stresses, and I can almost hear my heart racing.

Whatever the two of them are talking about seems to have a deeper meaning. Something bigger than the simple restaurant business.

"Nothing is going to happen if you just mind your own business. We had a deal. I am the one supposed to be taking care of this restaurant, and you people need to stay away from it. So, why are you constantly interfering?" Lorenzo demands, the frustration in his voice giving way to anger.

"I know what the deal was. But since you clearly can't manage this place on your own, the Ferraros thought it would be a good idea to intervene and help you. Which is all I am trying to do." The man tells him, a hint of jab and arrogance in his tone that only infuriates Lorenzo more.

"Oh, don't you start! You don't want to test me. I know what you did to Fitzwilliam. You think the Ferraros can protect you forever?" Lorenzo's tone becomes threatening, but his words seem to make me pause.

Fitzwilliam. Alistair.

Realization dawns on me, and I press a hand to my mouth to keep myself from gasping aloud. The Ferraro family. The name still sent shivers down my spine. I barely escaped the warehouse after Luca's warning, and now I knew for certain that Alistair's murder wasn't just about food or bad reviews. It was about something far more sinister.

"As a matter of fact, I do think the Ferraro family can protect me forever." I can hear the smirk of the man's voice as he talks, his every word hitting me like a blow. "You don't even understand how much power and influence that family has over this place. I can cut you some slack because you are new, but for the future, never make the mistake of threatening anyone who is linked with that family," he says, the warning clear in his voice.

"How powerful can they even be? If the people here and the authorities find out, you are all dead meat." Lorenzo says, but I can tell he is trying desperately to stay tough. The tremor in his voice is evident.

The man chuckles sarcastically, and I inch a little closer to see the view. He is shaking his head, looking at Lorenzo as if he is nothing more than an ignorant kid.

"You really are ignorant, aren't you?" he asks, raising an eyebrow at him. "The Ferraro family has run this town for generations. They don't operate out in the open, but they've always been here, pulling strings," he tells Lorenzo, his tone becoming serious as he continues.

"You have no idea how deep the history of this town goes. For ages, Cinque Terre has been the main hub for the most dangerous of businesses. The Ferraros took over this place when it was nothing more than a cluster of fishing villages and made it into their hub for smuggling all kinds of goods—wine, tobacco, even people sometimes—using these very waters." My eyes widen as I listen to him, unable to come to terms with everything that he is saying.

"You think the authorities can do anything to them? They cannot even touch that family because they are the ones that control everything. Tourists come here and think they're stepping into a quaint little village, but this place is as corrupt as any city. The Ferraros keep things quiet but make no mistake—they're in charge." He finishes, and I'm left there gaping.

"So, I will only give you this advice once. Don't mess with the Ferraros." he warns Lorenzo, "You already saw what happened to Alistair; you wouldn't want that to happen to *you* now, would you?"

I notice the expression on Lorenzo's face. He looks pale with a barely concealed look of fear as he shakes his head no.

"Good. I want to see these prices decrease before the Ferraros decide to withdraw their funds. I am sure there are other restaurants here that they can use to clean their money."

Just then I notice him turning around. I waste no time as I rush to a hiding spot, concealing myself from the view as I watch the man leave.

I stay there for a few more minutes, trying to come to terms with everything I just heard.

And just like that, we have a new twist in the already complicated story.

Chapter Twelve

Marco's Past

I bolt, feeling desperate to get out of the place as fast as I can. Everything that I just heard is ringing in my head as I rushed out of the restaurant. I have no idea where to go or what to do now.

After my experience in the warehouse, I knew I had become entangled in a dangerous situation. But the discovery of our town's deeply rooted history of corruption is a shock that is too much to absorb.

I keep running. Not even thinking about where I am going. I just know that I need to go somewhere away from here. Somewhere that I can think. How will I ever process everything I just heard?

The man's voice still rings in my head, and the words carry so much weight that I feel like I am drowning under them.

"Tourists come here and think they're stepping into a quaint little village, but this place is as corrupt as any city. The Ferraros keep things quiet but make no mistake—they're in charge."

I suddenly view my hometown—where I grew up and built a thriving career—in a disturbing new light. For the first time, I find myself wondering if delving into this case was a bad idea after all.

If I hadn't been so determined to uncover the truth, I never would have found out this information. Right now, I would much rather live in blissful ignorance than experience this sinking feeling. It makes me wonder just how many other secrets I don't know about this town.

But most importantly, what am I supposed to do with all this information? The suffocating nature of it is so complex that I fear there is no one I can trust. At the same time, I know I can't deal with this on my own.

Just then, I pause when I see a familiar figure standing nearby.

Marco's attention is focused intently on his phone. Just the sight of him is enough for me to relax, letting out a breath I didn't realize I had been holding.

He turns and notices me standing near him. The moment our eyes meet his expression shifts, and a wave of genuine concern washes over his face. I am sure I look disheveled after the way I ran out of the restaurant, and the shock of everything I just heard must still be evident on my face.

I watch as Marco immediately pockets the phone and makes his way to me in long, purposeful strides.

I hold my breath, anticipating the inevitable questions he will ask. Questions I have no idea how to answer. But as he approaches, he surprises me by pulling me into a hug, wrapping his arms around me as he holds me tightly.

I freeze, unsure of how to react. But the warmth of his embrace wears me down. After everything that I have just encountered, I can't help but melt in his arms, needing the comfort they bring.

Marco doesn't say anything for a moment, holding me close for a few minutes as if he needs to know I am there.

"Do you have any idea how worried I was?" his voice finally cuts through the air, pulling me out of my thoughts.

He pulls away a little to see my face. "I have been calling you for the past hour or so. Knowing that you were out meddling in dangerous business, I was going out of my mind with worry. Where were you?"

His fear for me is evident in his tone, and I can't ignore the way butterflies flutter in my stomach at his display of concern.

"I am sorry... I just..." I try to find the words to explain what just happened, but I look around and notice several people's attention on us. "Let's go somewhere else, and I will explain," I tell him, not wanting anyone to overhear us.

Marco senses my unease and doesn't question me. Nodding, he pulls back completely. We both walk quietly toward his empty bar. As soon as we enter, I take a deep breath, trying to let go of the nerves.

Marco locks the door after himself, understanding that whatever I am about to tell him is important enough that no one else should hear it.

I take a seat on one of the stools nearby. Instead of sitting beside me, he goes to the other side of the bar and pulls out two glasses, filling them before passing one to me.

I take it, raising an inquiring eyebrow at him as I look at the glass in confusion.

"I have a feeling we are going to need this," he says simply as he grabs his glass and comes to take a seat next to me, focusing all his attention on me. "Now spill."

I sigh, "I followed the new tourist. I have been keeping track of him. For some reason, he was always at Lorenzo's restaurant, and I dismissed it as nothing. But today..." I pause, still thinking about how I am supposed to tell him everything that I have learned. "I overheard a conversation between the two of them and found out that this town has many secrets I was unaware of."

An expression I don't recognize briefly crosses Marco's face.

"What do you mean?" he asks carefully.

I take a deep breath before recounting everything that has happened. I tell him about the Ferraro family and their role in Alistair's murder—how this entire town was built for their dirty work. I still have no idea how something so big has managed to stay a secret, but somehow, it did.

Once I finish telling him everything, I expect him to have a big reaction—to feel as disorientated as I felt when I first heard this. But unlike me, Marco sits there perfectly calm, as if I haven't told him anything new.

It takes me a moment to understand why. The realization leaves me feeling betrayed and shocked at the same time.

"You knew," I whisper, unable to swallow the bitterness of this reality. My only friend, the one person I had trusted, knew this and said nothing.

A guilty look crosses his features which only cements my suspicions further. I stare at him in disbelief.

"Look, it's not what you are thinking." Marco finally finds his voice, instantly trying to defend himself, but I shake my head, stopping him.

"Don't you dare say that? How can you defend this, Marco? I thought we were friends!" I say accusingly, my voice thick with emotions.

Regret flashes in his eyes at my words, and he shakes his head again.

"I am your friend. Please, just listen to me." He pleads, and even though I don't want to hear anything, I stay silent, giving him a chance to explain.

He notices my silence and takes it as an invitation for him to start talking.

"Remember when you asked me about my family, and I walked away? Well... this is all connected. I promise, I didn't mean to betray you, it's just that everything that I am involved in is too dangerous. I don't want to drag you into this mess," he explains, getting my attention instantly.

"What do you mean?" I ask, unable to connect the dots.

Marco sighs, taking one final deep breath before he finally comes clean, telling me about the past that he has spent so long trying to hide from everyone.

"My father... he was a chef in Cinque Terre, one of the best. He ran the finest restaurant in town, and for years, he was at the top of the list. But then... there was an incident," he pauses.

The pain in his voice makes my heart clench.

"There was a scandal," Marco continues. "My father had too many rivals, too many people who were trying to compete with him. And they found the perfect opportunity when a dish at a rival restaurant was poisoned, and my father was blamed. They said he sabotaged the competition, that he was trying to eliminate his rivals." Marco stops, and I can see how hard he is trying to keep himself together as he tells me this.

I don't ask him if it is true or not, letting him take a moment before he speaks again. But I am still unable to wrap my head around everything he just said.

In all the time I've known Marco, I never once saw something like this coming. He has always been the kind of person who didn't talk much about himself.

But only now do I understand why that is so. Just thinking of how terrible his childhood would have been makes my heart clench.

I am still not over the fact that he would keep something like this from me. Despite that, I can't help feeling bad for him. No child deserves this. Just the thought of what he must have gone through is difficult to imagine. But I know I am about to hear worse as he continues.

"It wasn't true. My father was the most honest person I knew. He would never do anything like that, but the accusations destroyed him. He lost everything—his reputation, the restaurant, and eventually... his life."

My breath catches in my throat at his words, my heart sinking as I realize how bad this is.

"Your father was framed?" I ask, unable to hide the sadness in my voice.

Marco nods, his face clouded with old pain. "He was innocent. But no one cared. The town turned on our family, and we had to leave Cinque Terre in disgrace. My father died heartbroken."

His voice sounds so painful that it pierces my heart.

"How old were you?" I ask gently, unsure of how to react to any of this.

"I was just ten. My family moved to a new town to start fresh, but I swore that I would clear his name one day. Which is why I came back here. I started digging. I reopened the restaurant and started the wine bar, but that was just a cover," he finally confesses, looking up to meet my eyes. "I've been quietly investigating my father's scandal, trying to find out who really sabotaged the dish and ruined his life,"

"And you think the Ferraros were involved?" I ask, piecing everything together.

"I don't know for sure," Marco admits. "But there is some connection. I started digging up the past, and that's how I crossed paths with Alistair. He was looking into the Ferraros as well. He found out something about the old case and was using it to extort someone. That's why they killed him."

My mind is spinning with everything I keep on learning. It's like somehow my whole world has been turned upside down in just one day. First, everything that I uncovered about this small town that I have always called my home. And now, Marco's past.

I try to find words, but I come up with nothing. He looks up at me expectantly, I try to pull myself together by locking my eyes with his.

"Why didn't you tell me any of this before?" I ask him softly, and the same guilty expression appears on his face.

"I couldn't risk it. If the Ferraros found out, it would put you in danger. That is the last thing I want to happen, Filomena," he says softly.

Even though my heart flutters at his words, I push the feeling away.

"I don't know, Marco. This is too big, and I have no idea what to say right now." I tell him honestly, trying to think clearly despite being extremely overwhelmed.

He nods understandingly before taking my hand in his and looking up into my eyes.

"I know that this isn't fair to you, and I should have told you sooner. I was afraid for your safety. But I promise you, Filomena, I have always been on your side. All along, my motive has been to find the real culprit, and I am still here to help you. Please give me a chance." He says, his tone pleading, and my heart tugs at me.

On one hand, I'm tempted to say no and tell him what he did was wrong. But on the other, a part of me can't help but sympathize with him. Not to mention that he has indeed been very willing to help with this case.

He continues looking at me expectantly, and eventually, I give in with a sigh.

"No more secrets," I warn him.

He nods instantly.

"Good, now let's get to the bottom of this case," I tell him.

He nods eagerly as we dive back into discussing the details. This time, we will put an end to this. Once and for all.

Chapter Thirteen

The Hidden Society

Marco and I stare at one another across the kitchen counter. He is waiting for me to say something while I'm mulling over my decision. He's here for a reason—a vital cause, the green light I needed to discover the truth.

"I've got this!" Heaving a sigh, I finally announce my decision, more for myself than him. I can't say I'm not scared to take such a giant leap toward the unknown. I grab my coat and put it on, clutching the note he has given me—the crucial clue I needed to execute my wild schemes.

"I still suggest you reconsider this, Filomena. This plan is not safe at all," his face contorted with deep concern, his eyebrows furrowed.

But I have made my decision. There's no going back. I can't stop now when I'm this close to unmasking the secret that has engulfed the town for so long.

"You should know better than to downplay my abilities, Marco. I'll reach the roots of the evil, and nothing can stop me," I tell him with a chuckle, even though I'm trembling with doubt from inside.

His lips stretch into a smile as he shakes his head. He knows that I'm unstoppable when I put my mind to something.

"Just promise me you'll take care of yourself, OK?" He utters softly.

My heart warms at the look of concern in his eyes. I nod and smile as I wave at him and exit the restaurant.

Once outside, my pulse quickens as I stare at the note provided by Marco. It took incredible effort, time, and energy to find this crucial clue through his connections and ties. If it weren't for him, I wouldn't have had this important lead that would help me discover the dark secrets.

I have no time to waste! From the information Marco has provided, there's going to be a high stakes meeting of *La Tavola Segreta*. No exact location, no name—just a vague address where the restaurant is located. I guess I'll have to find out by myself.

"Let's get going, Pepperoni. We have a veiled secret to uncover—probably the biggest secret surrounding this town." Tugging at his leash, I murmur to my partner in crime as I begin the journey toward the harbour front.

They have chosen a perfect time—as if ashamed to conduct their shady activities in the morning light.

On our way, Pepperoni is busy sniffing anything he finds interesting. The little furball has always been my steady figure in turmoil. Giving him a gentle pat, I tilt the brim of my cap lower to hide my face in case any involved members recognize me. I have to be careful because the whole town knows what I am after—*who* I'm after.

I walk for a few more minutes with Pepperoni fast on my tail, but I stop dead in my tracks as I reach the provided address. *Oh, my...!* How can I figure out which restaurant is going to host the meeting? There's a whole market here! Unfolding the paper in my hand, I squint my eyes to read the address more carefully in case I missed something, but there's nothing. The only direction provided in the note is the right side of the harbour front. As I approach, I find three restaurants in a row.

Scanning the crowded market, I'm still debating on what to do when my eyes fall upon an alley.

My heart starts pulsating and a sick feeling forms in my stomach as I stare at the secluded passage; its lack of light adds to the eerie atmosphere.

But there's no restaurant here. The note states that the meeting is inside a restaurant.

My eyes are still surveying the marketplace when I spot a familiar figure, walking briskly and glancing nervously from side to side. I need to get closer to be sure, but the tight bun and the cold demeanor tell me I know who it is. My eyes widen as I finally see her face and confirm my suspicion.

Giovanna.

Her measured approach and cautious aura leave me to believe that she is here for the private meeting.

She enters one of the restaurants named "Casa di Pasta". The lavish, vintage exterior of the restaurant tells a story about its historical significance. I know about this restaurant. The owner, Filippo Moretti is a well-known businessman in Cinque Terre. Of all the restaurants in town, I never would have guessed this would be the one I was seeking.

Does it mean he is also one of the members? Another surprise of the night!

I rack my brain trying to figure out how to enter the restaurant without being seen. If I am discovered, this investigation is over.

Think, Filomena. Think!

As I'm trying to figure out what to do, Pepperoni dashes forward, his leash slipping out of my hand.

"Pepperoni!" I call out from behind him as I sprint forward to get a hold of him.

Oh, no! He can't run, not now when I'm on the verge of discovering the truth. I don't have time for this. I have to get in there to see what's happening.

Frustrated, I run after Pepperoni who lets out an enthusiastic woof. At least, someone is enjoying the evening while here I am on the verge of pulling my hair out. Time is ticking, and I'm running behind my dog who has no plans to stop.

He runs inside the same alleyway that I was staring at earlier.

"Pepperoni, no! Stop!" I call out but to no avail. I wish he had chosen some other time for his games—when I'm not this close to discovering what's really going on here.

He lets out another woof, ignoring me completely. Stretching my hand toward his leash, I try to grab it, but he races off and darts through a slim door.

The feelings in this alley are not sitting well in my gut, now I have to go into this door.

Without a choice, I follow him inside and find him descending a narrow staircase. It looks like some kind of underground building—dark, quiet, secretive, and... intriguing.

Despite the fear etched in my chest, I follow Pepperoni down the stairs and find him at the bottom, sniffing at a piece of bread. Running my eyes around the area, I find a vaulted stone cellar that's illuminated by a bulb hanging on the wall. A wine cellar? But... why is it so shady?

"Here you are!" I pick Pepperoni up in my arms, trying to shake the uneasy feeling that has settled in my chest. He's now munching on the piece of bread.

I'm about to leave the cellar when I hear voices—arguments to be specific. They seem to be coming from the cellar door that is slightly ajar. I have more important things to do, but something tells me I should stay.

Taking a deep breath, I place Pepperoni down and run my hand along his back. "Shh! You have to be quiet," I whisper. Pepperoni's face scrunches up, showing that he understands what I'm trying to tell him.

I peek through the doorway slightly, trying to hide my face. As soon as I do, my mouth drops to the floor.

There's a large wooden table surrounded by some of the most influential people in the town. I know them. I know them all very well...

Among the familiar faces, I spot Giovanna's scowl as she listens to Fransesco, a famous wine distributor. To say that I'm shocked would be an understatement.

If the so-called meeting is being held in this shady wine cellar, why did I clearly see Giovanna go into Casa di Pasta earlier? Could I be wrong? No, I am sure I saw her.

This cellar must be connected to the restaurant somehow. My eyes widen even more as the realization dawns upon me. Did Pepperoni just... unknowingly lead me right into their meeting?

My heart warms as I cast an appreciative glance at Pepperoni, who is busy munching on the piece of bread once again. What did I do to deserve him?

Refocusing my attention back to the meeting, I listen intently to what's being said. The atmosphere is thick with tension as everyone shares their two cents.

I'm still in disbelief at all the esteemed individuals sitting around the table, wearing solemn expressions. Restaurant owners like Giovanna, wealthy patrons like Fransesco, and Serena Esposito, a chef I've looked up to all my life... they all are part of this big secret.

There are documents and papers on the table and a black ledger that must contain some key information.

I notice something else—they all are wearing a silver ring. Squinting my eyes to take a closer look, my whole body stills. It's the same ring I noticed on Giovanna's forefinger when I went to her restaurant the other day to confront her—a fork and a knife engraved on a black shining stone in a cross style. How foolish of me to think that the ring represented her passion for cooking!

Such a wise conclusion, Filomena!

Can it be a symbol for this secret society?

"Alistair was a risk we couldn't afford. We had to get rid of him. There was no choice. The Ferraros ordered me to get rid of him," Fransesco's deep, somber voice fills my ears, his eyes dark and dangerous. I have met him a couple of times to purchase wine for my restaurant. I have never seen this intense side of him.

Oh, the Ferraros!

My heart starts racing at the mention of Alistair's name. We are finally getting somewhere.

"I have heard that someone is on our tail for the same reason. What if they get a whiff of the society's purpose? Do you think we can afford that? I still think that removing Alistair from the scene was a terrible idea!" Sophia, a renowned local food manufacturer says with a tone that can cut the air.

Their faces twist with realization and dissent.

"We have taken care of Luca. There is no need to panic. No one can track it back to us." It's Giovanna this time who has spoken with her usual curt tone.

What does she mean by "taking care" of Luca? Have they murdered him too?

My breathing quickens as I keep listening.

"What's done is done. Besides, Alistair wouldn't keep his nose out of our business, and Luca knew too much. Do you think we could just let them live and expose us? Not only that, but they also knew about Jacob." My mind races as I hear them confess to their crimes.

Jacob? Marco's father?

My stomach churns with disgust. I can't believe what I'm hearing. It means my suspicion was right. They have killed them! Here I am, peeking through the door, a witness as they confess their crimes. *La Tavola Segreta* holds the key to all the dirty secrets of the town—Alistair's murder and now Luca's. Even the allegations against Marco's father are all connected to this clandestine society.

I'm still listening to them when suddenly, Pepperoni lets out a "woof". My eyes widen as I snap my head towards Pepperoni who's looking at me questioningly.

My gaze darts toward the meeting room where a silence has fallen upon it. Nobody speaks a word as their anxious gazes slowly turn to the source of the sound.

"Who's there?" Fransesco's cautious yet sharp voice hits my ears. My heart starts racing when I see him dash toward the door. Oh, shoot! I'm trapped!

I know that I can't run now even if I try to, so I make the most impulsive move of my life. I open the door before he can do so and step inside from my hiding spot, with my chin held high.

They all look at me like they're seeing a ghost. I hear shocked gasps as they stand up.

"I know everything. I have already recorded everything and forwarded the footage, so don't try to intimidate me." I lie through clenched teeth, but what can I do?

"I am aware of your role in Alistair's death as well as the false allegations you made against Marco's father, and now Luca too. You thought you could get away with your heinous crimes while shielding yourselves behind *La Tavola Segreta?* A secret society? Seriously?" I shake my head as I grace each one of them with a disgusted stare.

They exchange panicked looks as the room fills with a tense silence. Nobody seems to know what to do when, finally, Fransesco's sharp voice cuts through the air.

I infer that he is the leader of the society.

"Stop meddling with our business, woman! People who have interfered previously have either disappeared from the surface of the earth or are living a miserable life. I wouldn't have involved myself if I were you." His loud, intimidating voice inflicts a shiver down my spine, but I hold my ground. His furious gaze fixates on me as he warns me.

All the scared faces in the room look between Fransesco and me.

"I told you that you won't intimidate me. I'm going to expose you all along with your dirty secrets. I will not allow harm to the town where I have lived my whole life. I won't let you ruin any more lives!" My chest rises and falls in quick rhythms, and my ears ring as I breathe heavily after lashing out.

"Do you know what will happen to Marco if you expose us? He'll be ruined just like his father. Poor guy! He must not be aware that the woman he treasures doesn't care about him at all!" Giovanna steps in, folding her arms across her chest as she graces me with a pitiful look. She's trying to emotionally blackmail me with Marco, and for a moment, her tactics are successful.

My decision wavers for a second as I think about what she has said, but I know what I should do. She can't manipulate me. I know them well enough to know they'll do anything to stop me.

"Nothing will happen to him. His father, Alistair, and Luca deserve justice," I say in a calm and determined voice, keeping my chin high.

It all happens in the blink of an eye. Suddenly, Fransesco lunges forward and yanks my arm. I shriek as I try to free myself from his tight grip. I can smell his putrid breath as he grabs my arms tightly and stares angrily into my eyes.

He frees one of my arms and raises his hand to strike me. Anticipating the blow, I close my eyes. But before his fist connects, Pepperoni lets out an angry bark and rushes toward him, attaching himself to Fransesco's leg with his sharp teeth.

Startled by the sudden attack, Fransesco lets out a hiss and finally releases me.

Amidst the chaos, I quickly grab the black ledger from the table. I don't know what I'm holding, but I know it's something significant.

Pepperoni continues barking and attacking Fransesco who's frantically trying to save himself. The others stand in shock. Grabbing his leash, I dart for the door and run toward the stairs. There's panic in the room as everyone starts yelling at once and rushing after me.

I don't stop. I don't look back. My only focus is on escaping, knowing they will kill me in a heartbeat if they catch me.

The shouting continues behind me, but I don't slow my pace. With Pepperoni close behind me and the ledger clutched tightly in my hand, I sprint down the alleyway toward the market.

Don't give up! Don't stop, Filomena!

I encourage myself to keep going. I run until I find another alleyway. I sneak a quick look to see if they're still chasing after me, but the crowded market slows them down. I bump and push past people until I reach the alleyway where I know they won't see me hiding.

Beside the alleyway, I spot an empty shop. I quickly duck into the shopfront and cast a backward glance, relieved to find the coast is clear.

Leaning against the wall, I try to calm my frantic heartbeat. Blood is pumping through my ears as I slowly slide down the wall to the floor, exhausted from running. Pepperoni joins me. The ledger is still tightly clutched in my arms. I glance at the ledger wondering what ugly truths about *La Tavola Segreta* it might hold.

With trembling hands, I open it and quickly scan its pages. Pepperoni settles on my lap, licking my face. He's truly a remarkable hero in my story. Kissing his head, I refocus my attention on the ledger.

My eyes widen as I soak in the contents: details of Jacob, Luca and Alistair, money laundering, and illegal trade. Every entry boasts proud confessions of crimes that have enveloped the town for ages.

As I turn the last page, I let out a sharp gasp.

I was going to be their next target. I *am* going to be their next target.

Chapter Fourteen

Intensifying Doubts

I stare blankly at the ceiling while my mind races with all kinds of scenarios—all the favorable and adverse outcomes I can think of.

It's been two days since the chaotic events—two days since I discovered the painful secrets about *La Tavola Segreta,* about the town, and about the lives they have destroyed.

And, about the fact that they have plans to get rid of me...

I haven't been at peace since. I haven't gone to La Nonna's Nonna. I haven't talked to anyone, including Marco.

He has been constantly calling me and texting me to know what has happened. He knew that I was going into the lion's den—knew that I would be in danger. Maybe, that's why he has been frantic trying to check on me.

To help him ease up, I text him that I'm alright and just need time.

And I took two days!

Now, I'm sprawled on my favorite couch while I try to decide what to do. I am constantly on edge, my mind whirling. I should've recorded them like I claimed when I had the chance. But for some reason, I wasn't thinking.

I still can't think straight. I'm fixated on what I heard, and everyone involved, not to mention all the confessions.

To be honest, I'm not just a little shaken. I'm truly terrified. These are perilous people. I now know they'll stop at nothing to keep their "little" society a secret. I have no doubt that I would face the same fate as Alistair and Luca—*especially* after I read the ledger.

Filomena. I can still see my name written in the ledger. They want me gone!

I don't know what to do. I can't let fear stand in my way. The well-being of the whole town of Cinque Terre is in my hands. This ledger is the proof I need to expose the corruption of the esteemed Ferraro family and the schemes of *La Tavola Segreta.*

But will the police take action against them, or do they have the law in their pockets? Nobody raises an eyebrow in front of them. Do I stand a chance against such filthy, powerful people?

I sigh, getting up from the couch and going to fetch the ledger. On my way, I find Pepperoni playing with his frisbee.

"Hey, Pepperoni, what should I do? You're such a brave boy for helping me the other day! Should I report them to the police?" Crouching down, I ask Pepperoni in a helpless voice.

He wiggles his tail excitedly as he listens to me, making it seem like he's answering my question by telling me to go ahead.

I go to the kitchen to pour myself a glass of water. I stand under the dim light of the kitchen with the soft hum of the refrigerator filling the room, feeling the weight of the impending decisions. I need to calm my mind before deciding. I can only hide for so long.

I'm busy sipping water when something clicks.

Placing the glass on the counter with a loud thud, I dash for my room, quickly open the drawer that holds the ledger, and flip through the pages.

A gasp escapes my lips as I stare at the words.

Ricci.

For days now, I had feared that Ricci was caught up in this to some extent, but I hadn't considered that he could be a threat to the Ferraros. With the diligence he has put into investigating Alistair's case, he inevitably has some clues that they're afraid of.

Now I am confident that Constable Ricci will help me expose these criminals.

Chapter Fifteen

The Final Choice

Five Months Later

The clinking of silverware and the soft murmurs are creating the usual buzz in La Nonna's Nonna. The servers are navigating the crowded restaurant with practiced agility. Things are back to normal, but what's not normal is the number of reservations we receive during the lunch and dinner hours.

I have been quite overwhelmed with the attention La Nonna's Nonna has received for the past five months. My little cozy restaurant has turned into a favorite savory nook for the townspeople and the tourists. The warm weather has drawn the tourists like flies to honey.

The booming tourist season is not the only factor behind La Nonna's Nonna's success. The real catalyst for its prosperity is what happened five months ago—the demise of the Ferraro Family.

Once again, I am called a hero, the savior of the town. It feels surreal. My motivation in exposing the corruption wasn't to become a celebrity chef. It was out of fierce loyalty to the town I call "home."

After what feels like hours, the restaurant finally calms as the dinner hour elapses.

"Maria, I'm stepping out for a bit. Will be back within an hour. Please cover for me until then," I request as I read the text I received a moment ago.

"Sure. Meeting Marco, I'm guessing?" Her voice holds a tinge of mischief as she wiggles her eyebrows.

"How did you know?" I ask, unable to remove the smile from my face.

"The smile says it all," she shrugs with a chuckle and leaves to take care of the business.

Feeling giddy, I leave the restaurant and walk toward the beach, taking in the colorful sunset that spreads across the sky. As the sun's light fades along with the chaos of the day, it creates a serene sanctuary—our favorite scenario for our rendezvous. I chuckle remembering how angry I was when he left so abruptly the first time we met here.

At the time, I was really taken aback by his response to my questions about his family. Now, I understand, and without his digging into the secret society, I never would have been able to uncover the truth.

When I first approached Ricci with my suspicions, he didn't seem eager to entertain the idea. However, when I showed him the ledger and pointed out the society's upcoming missions, he was furious. He was especially furious to read their plan to remove him from his post.

And so, after a month of secretly planning and investigating, he was finally able to catch them. The Ferraro family's demise wasn't easy to bring about but watching them be brought to justice gave me a deep feeling of satisfaction.

As I reach the beach, the salty aroma fills my nostrils, and my lips stretch into a wide grin. I'm enjoying the cool breeze on my face and the captivating landscape before me when I feel a pair of strong arms engulf me from behind. A surprised gasp escapes my lips. Turning around, I take in Marco's smiling face.

"Marco? You scared me!" I chuckle lightly.

"Who else would it be? I can't believe that the woman who plays detective and confronts dangerous criminals is scared of me," his eyes twinkle as he teases me.

I shake my head. "I'm not scared of you. I was just distracted for a moment, and you caught me off guard! Filomena being scared? No chance!"

He just smiles as we stroll along the beach side by side, enjoying the tranquility of the crashing waves and the comforting feel of his hand in mine.

It feels surreal...

"How's La Nonna's Nonna doing?" He asks after a while.

"Don't even ask! I haven't had a second to breathe all day because we have been so busy," I inform him wearily.

"It's no wonder. People are quite curious about the person who exposed such a big secret in the town. I'm sure you're happy about it—I mean, the success," he says chuckling.

"Of course!" I answer with a happy smile. "But, what I'm really happy about is the fact that the town is finally safe. It truly makes me happy that I could contribute to this peace."

"I'm glad. Now that everything's back to normal, I want to ask you something." He stops midway.

I stop beside him, looking up at him in confusion.

He stares at me hesitantly, slowly bringing his hands forward to grab mine.

"I have been meaning to confess how I feel, but with everything going on, there wasn't a good chance to do this. I have grown a profound liking for you, Filomena. From the first day I saw you, I have found you to be captivating. You have my heart. Will you consider being my girlfriend?"

I stare at him at a loss for words, distracted by the butterflies in my stomach.

He gazes back at me with an unsure expression on his face, worrying what my answer will be.

"Yes! Of course!" I say in a breathy tone.

His face lights up as he hears my answer. He grabs me in his arms and spins me around, prompting me to let out a joyful giggle.

Could the night be any more perfect?

Could my life be any more perfect?

Printed in Great Britain
by Amazon